BRIGHT LIGHTS FROM A HURRICANE

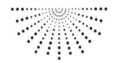

ALSO BY GRACE MCGINTY

Hell's Redemption Trilogy

The Redeemable

The Unrepentant

The Fallen

The Azar Trilogy (coming 2019)

Smoke and Smolder

Burn and Blaze

Rage and Ruin

Stand Alone Novels and Novellas

Bright Lights From A Hurricane

The Last Note (coming 2019)

Treasure

The Castle of Carnal Desires

BRIGHT LIGHTS FROM A HURRICANE

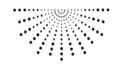

GRACE MCGINTY

ISBN: 978-0-6484757-0-5 (paperback)

ISBN: 978-0-6484757-1-2 (eBook)

To those who support me and my crazy life choices. This is for you, always.

CHAPTER ONE

LAKE CITY, FLORIDA

Hellson *Brothers Amusements accepts no responsibility in the event of injury or Death.*

My heart thumped hard against my ribs at the word "Death". They'd even capitalized the D, in case you didn't fully comprehend the seriousness of the word. I held the small red ticket so tightly that my knuckles were starting to ache, and I could feel the blood rushing away from my face. The fine print on the back of the ticket felt like the call of a banshee.

This was a bad idea. No, this was worse than bad, this was a horrendous idea. In my other hand I clutched a small black Moleskine journal. Looking at its pretty gold embossing gave me strength. Despite the chance of death with a capital D, I had to do this.

Pale faced teenagers stumbled out of the ride's

exit gate, some looking exhilarated, the rush of adrenaline still coursing through their bodies like a natural high, but others looked more shell-shocked and green. One kid burst out of the barrier gate and only made it a few steps before he lost what appeared to be a barely masticated corn dog, and judging by the color, pink cotton candy. I looked away quickly before my own stomach revolted in sympathy. The carnival worker opened the 'IN' gate, and everyone lined up to enter.

Hell's Hurricane. It was the most popular ride at the carnival every year, but I wasn't sure why. From what I'd observed as I stood here for the last hour, trying to force myself to buy a ticket, you were strapped into a seat with a harness that didn't look nearly safe enough, then you began to spin at a high velocity, and if that wasn't enough, you were flung eighty or so feet in the air back and forth like a pendulum until you were essentially upside down. Why anyone would subject themselves to this voluntarily was beyond me, but I was going to be one of those senseless people. I had to do it. I had a promise to keep. My best friend Angela and I watched people ride it every year, and every year she'd beg me to go on it with her. Every year I refused. I liked being alive, thank you very much. I wasn't going to be a late night headline.

I sucked in a deep breath and stepped up to the gate.

"Only one?"

I nodded. The guy took my ticket, and waved me through. He had bright blue eyes that flashed with the strobe lights of the ride.

I paused just inside the gate and bit my lip, a nervous habit I'd had for as long as I could remember. "Can I have that ticket back? I promise not to try and ride again." I dragged my eyes away from his face and stared at my feet. "I just really need it."

The guy searched my face, probably taking in my already pasty complexion and the note of desperation in my voice, but he nodded.

"Okay. But I'll write void on it and then give it back to you after the rides over." He tucked it into the chest pocket of his polo shirt. I gave him a tight smile. That was good enough.

I walked to an empty seat and sat down. I tucked the moleskine journal into the inside pocket of my leather jacket and then zipped it up tight. My purse and phone were already securely tucked away. I pulled the harness down until it clicked. And that was it. All my safety rested on the secureness of a single latch.

My breathing was shallow and my hands were clammy. I pictured Angela's face, telling me that I was a scaredy cat, that I never did anything even a little adventurous, and it made me more resolute. I took a deep breath, counted to ten and let it back out again. I could do this. The carnie with the blue eyes came over and pushed and pulled at my harness, checking it was secure before continuing down the line of people.

Finally the ride started, and I closed my eyes against the blur of lights and faces. It began to sway gently at first, but I could feel the arm swinging more violently outwards with each pass, moving higher and higher into the air. My stomach was already in knots, and every downward drop pushed my heart up into my throat. People started to scream, and I could feel my own fear filling my lungs with girlish squeals.

I held onto the bars for dear life, but that didn't stop me from slipping and sliding around in the harness. Logic tried to convince me that I wasn't going to slip out unless I somehow turned into a liquid, but every other part of my brain screamed that I was going to die. My throat hurt, and that's when I realized I was screaming into the night right along with everyone else. The pendulum reached the peak of its ascent, and time seemed to stand still as gravity took us in her terrifying hands.

"Look, Livvy. It doesn't count if you don't look,"

Angela's voice whispered in my mind. I pried open my eyelids one by one, and looked. I could see the whole carnival, and most of the town from this height. I made the mistake of looking directly at the ground and my stomach whirled as I slammed my eyes shut again.

After what felt like the longest three minutes of my life, the ride finally started to slow, until it came to a complete stop. I wanted to race out of the seat and back onto solid ground, but I couldn't move, couldn't get my hands to release the bars. I couldn't even open my eyes. I was frozen.

Someone touched my arm. "Hey, are you okay?"

I shook my head and kept my eyes closed. I was so far from okay, I wasn't even in the same hemisphere anymore. I hadn't been okay for weeks. The blue eyed carnie, I'd recognized his voice, gently pried my hands off of the bars of the harness and raised it over my head. He put one hand under my elbow, and helped me to my feet. My legs wobbled and I almost landed face first on the metal flooring.

"Woah, steady there. Come on, I'll help you down the stairs. I haven't done your ticket yet, but I'm going on a break anyway so I'll do it now." He lead me down the stairs like I was eighty instead of eighteen and over to the ticket box.

"Ted, pass me a pen will you?" The grizzled old

guy in the ticket booth threw a pen over his shoulder without even looking. Blue Eyes plucked it from the air with ease and leaned up against the booth, writing "VOID" over the fine print on the back of the ticket. "Here you go. You still look shaky, where are you friends? I'll make sure you get there without falling on your face."

"I didn't come with anyone." My voice sounded rough; I'd probably strained it with all the petrified screaming I'd been doing. Blue Eyes looked at me and frowned. Yep, he was cute and now he knew I was a loser. Great. He had dark blonde hair peeking out from under a hat, and a tank top that exposed way too much tanned muscle for my brain to compose anything resembling witty conversation.

"I'll grab you a bottle of aqua until you look a little less like death then." I flinched at the word but nodded. He led me to a food van and went around to the side door. "Hey Dolly, can I grab a couple of bottles of water?" A plump woman, about sixty, looked up from a deep fryer and smiled at Blue Eyes. She reached into the fridge under the counter and pulled out two bottles of water and threw them at us. Apparently, no one politely passed anything within the carnival. "Here you go, Sugar. How's Hurricane going tonight?"

"It's a little slow, but not too bad for the last night of the carnival. Later."

He led me to the back of the van, where there was a small green plastic table and some fold up chairs. He pushed down on my shoulders and sat me in the chair, handing me the drink like an invalid. "Here. Now drink."

Because I'd been raised with good manners, I did what I was told. He took the chair opposite me. We sat in silence for a little while, and I realized I still had the ticket in my hand. I unzipped my jacket and pulled out the journal. I skipped to the correct page, and tucked the ticket into the little pocket that had been pasted there.

Blue Eyes watched the ritual without speaking, until I slid the book back into my jacket.

"Was that a diary?"

I stared at the dirt patch where the fall of hundreds of shoes had worn away the grass. "Kind of. It's a bucket list."

He smiled, and his teeth were straight and white. "You wrote a bucket list that had The Hurricane on it?" He seemed surprised, and judging by my impression of a statue at the end of the ride, I guess he'd gathered I wasn't exactly a thrill-seeker.

"No, it's my best friend's bucket list."

"Was she too afraid to do it herself?" he laughed.

"No, she's dead. Aggressive brain cancer. She never got to complete even half of it." I said this emotionlessly, because if I let even a scrap of emotion through, I was going to lose it all, right here, in front of Blue Eyes.

"Shit. I'm sorry." He shifted uncomfortably, his tongue darting out to wet his lower lip, before dragging it between his teeth. "So you are doing her bucket list for her?" I nodded, still not meeting his eyes; besides that thing he did with his lip was a little mesmerizing and I was a little afraid I'd stare. "May I see?"

That made me look at him. I studied his face, but all I saw was empathy. I passed him the journal from my pocket. He opened it to the first page, and there was a picture of Angela, laughing at the camera. The first few things had been easy. Drive a car at a 130 miles per hour. Eat dessert for every meal for a day. Dance on a bar. Do an open mic night. Write letters to everyone she loved. Egg Heidi Summer's house. We'd done all those things together. Angela living her life, and me behind the camera taking pictures.

"She looks like she was a lot of fun." He was looking at the picture I'd taken of her dancing on the bar. Angela had been beautiful and kind, friendly to everyone she met, but she was a little wild too. She had mischievous streak a mile wide. To this day, I don't know how we became friends. I was reserved, quiet even. I only ever crossed the street at pedestrian crossings. I did all my homework and listened to my parents. Angela had done things like climb onto her roof to watch the sunrise or borrow her mother's car in the middle of the night to drive to Wendy's for a burger. But everyone had loved her, her joy was infectious.

"She believed in living life to the fullest. She said there is no point playing on the safe side, because you never know when the zombie apocalypse might happen. She was funny like that." A smile crept onto my face. Angela would have loved the boy in front of me. He was exactly her type. Well, he was everyones type unless you were allergic to broad, blonde and sexy.

"The next thing on the list says 'Have a Grand Adventure'. What are you planning to do for that?"

I shrugged. I had no idea what Angela's version of a grand adventure was, but I was one hundred percent sure our definitions varied dramatically. To me, buying my clothes online was a grand adventure.

"Why don't you join the carnival? You're eighteen right? We criss-cross our way down through the Deep South for the summer and then we go our separate ways during winter. It's like four months, tops. Nothing says grand adventure like running away to join the carnival. And we have a place open right now. My sister, Liz, just had a baby and she's… unwell. We've been covering her booth but we are all stretched a little thin." His jaw tensed slightly, and I had the immediate impression that there was more to the story than Blue Eyes let on.

I stared at him, my jaw swinging open. Could I do that? Just leave everyone behind, put off college prep, and become a carnie for four months? My parents would kill me. I didn't know these people and had no idea about how to work in a carnival surrounded by strangers. What if they dumped my body in some Louisiana bayou?

I looked at the bright, flashing lights, and breathed in the deep fried smell of corn dogs and doughnuts. What would Angela do?

That one was easy.

"Okay. I'll do it." It came out as a squeak.

Blue Eyes grinned. "Well, that's great. I'll talk to Ruben, he's my brother and the manager, and tell him you'll be joining us. This is like kismet or something," he said laughingly. "We head out first thing Tuesday morning for Madison. Here, I'll put my number in your phone. Give me a call and we'll arrange everything. I'm Dallas Hellson by the way." I knew he was giving me time to sleep on it, to overthink it to death, but I didn't need a cooling off period. My mind was made up. All grand adventures started with just closing your eyes and taking a leap of faith.

"Olivia Jefferson. I'll see you on Tuesday." I shook his hand. I'd just accepted a job offer from a guy before I even knew his name.

"Welcome to the Hellson Brothers Carnival, Olivia. I hope you are ready for an adventure."

Excitement ran over me in a wave. But first I had to tell my parents.

CHAPTER TWO

LAKE CITY, FLORIDA

My father's shouts were a testament to how angry he was. In all my eighteen years, I'd never heard him raise his voice. Not because he was a doting parent, but because my father believed that stoicism was next to godliness. Plus, it was hard to be mad if you were never home much.

To be honest, I'd never given him any cause to raise his voice. I'd always been studious, respectful, and most importantly to my parents, quiet. Always seen and not heard.

Mother wasn't shouting, just looking at me with quizzical disappointment, like I was one of her experiments that had suddenly failed, and she was trying to find the exact point in her scientific method when things had started to go wrong.

I could answer that for her, though; the parenthood experiment began to go wrong at the conception stage. I'd known for a long time that my parents should never have reproduced. They were both professionals, my father a hugely successful corporate lawyer and my mother was a pharmaceutical researcher. We lived in an oversized, opulent house, but it was always empty. Just me and an assortment of housekeepers until I was old enough to care for myself, which in my parent's opinion, was at the age of eight. Our house was the biggest on the block, its interior designed by the best firm in Lake City. But it was never a home.

I hadn't realized that there was a difference until Junior High, when Angela had adopted me like a neglected puppy. She'd taken me home one day after school and as soon as I'd stepped through the door in their simple, single story bungalow, I'd had that epiphany. The sudden realization that my life wasn't the same as everyone else's.

Love permeated every corner of Angela's house. She'd been an IVF baby, and her parents had nearly bankrupted themselves trying for a child, so when she'd been born, they'd forgotten every heartache, every ounce of anguish and every other responsibility they had just to dote on their perfect baby girl. At least, that's what Angela's mom said when she told the story of how Angela was born. It was a story they told often, and Angela would roll her eyes in embarrassment, but I listened intently for every second of the story. Not because I couldn't repeat it verbatim in the end, but because I was always entranced by the look of utter love and adoration on her mom's face.

They'd had so much love in their hearts, and they'd taken one look at me, so reserved and quiet, and they'd adopted me too. For years, they'd treated me like a second child, and during my teen years, I'd spent so much time at their house they'd started calling their guest room "Livvy's Room".

Angela's mom, Lindy, had given me my first hug, had gushed over my report cards, and Angela had consoled me when I didn't get a date for Junior Prom. They became my family. At first my parents hadn't noticed, they never came home before nine p.m. anyway, and later I think they were secretly relieved that they didn't have to "parent" anymore. As long as I got good grades, and smiled dutifully when their bosses came over for dinner parties, they didn't care how I spent my days.

In fact, it had been Angela's parents that I had called first about my job offer.

Angela's parents were ghosts of their former vibrant selves since Angela's death. I'd heard her dad whimper into his wife's chest, asking God what he'd done so wrong, why they'd worked so hard to get their angel, only to have her taken away by an invisible monster that they couldn't fight. It had been heartbreaking, but when you see someone that exposed, and they have seen you similarly laid bare, you are closer than any ties of blood.

So when I called and told them I was "running away to join the carnival", they worried. Because that's what people who love you do when you commit to something outrageous.

"Are you sure it's safe?" Tom, Angela's dad, had asked. He was a big, burly guy, who worked in construction and had a weathered face from being outside all the time. But the laugh lines around his eyes were like estuaries, and he was still quite handsome in a salt of the earth kind of way.

I assured them that it was perfectly safe, even though I had no idea if that were true or not. I didn't want them to worry. Then they asked about school, and the plans I had for an internship at my father's firm over the summer.

"I got an offer for Stanford." And Yale. And Harvard. They didn't need to know that, though. I hadn't been able to decide, well, anything. But this felt right.

"Oh my goodness, well done Livvy. We are so proud!"

They honestly were, I knew that. But I could hear the pain that tightened Lindy's voice, and the guilt overshadowing Tom's own congratulations. They were happy for me, but it was tarnished. I knew that no matter how pleased they were, I would always be a measuring stick by which they could tell all the milestones they would miss in Angela's life. It was with Angela that they should be celebrating college acceptances, and Angela that they should be waving off on a big adventure to higher education. And deep down, because they were good people, I knew they felt guilty that they couldn't share my good news without feeling sad. Because, despite everything, they loved me too.

If anything, it made me more resolute to go on this wild ride. To accept Stanford. A grand adventure. We all needed the time and space to try to heal.

"I'll get to Stanford in time for orientation. And besides, I don't even want to be a lawyer. I want to go to medical school. Father set up the internship, not me. I need to do this."

There was a long, heavy silence at the other end of the phone, and I breathed a sigh of relief when they gave me their blessing, as long as I promised to call every couple of days, but preferably every day. If

I was honest, if they'd told me to stay, I would have. I'd move mountains not to cause them any more pain. I owed them and Angela so much.

But they'd let me go, as I knew they would. They understood better than anyone else why I had to do this.

However, then came the reality of my own parents.

Father's face was turning a weird, mottled grey, and I was worried that he might have a stroke.

"If you do this Olivia, don't bother coming back," he shouted. "Do you know how hard I worked to get you that internship? They'd wanted to give it to Johansson's pea-brained son. Little did I know my own daughter would have such little sense herself."

I pulled my bag towards the front door, ignoring his tirade. I'd thrown whatever I could in a bag, my prized possessions and some clothes. The photos of Angela and me. The teddy she and her family had given me when they'd realized that I'd never had any toy that wasn't educational. Velvet the Bunny had been my secret companion when I'd had to return home, and I hugged her close every night before hiding her in my closet every morning.

"Are you even listening to me, Olivia? I mean it, young lady. I will cut you off, disinherit you in a heartbeat."

"Yes, Father." I pulled the door closed softly behind me. Old habits die hard, as they say.

The door was wrenched open again. "I can get a court order, I can make you stay," he fumed.

"I'm eighteen, Father. I turned eighteen last month. You guys just forgot." And that had hurt, despite the fact that I hadn't expected them to remember. My birthday had gone unremarked, because my parents had forgotten, and my surrogate parents were wrapped in a cloud of grief. I didn't mind, I hadn't felt like celebrating anyway.

He didn't have the good grace to look embarrassed that he'd forgotten his only child's birthday, but I was saved from the rest of his tirade by Dallas pulling into the driveway. Right on time, bless him.

Father took one look at Dallas' beat up pickup truck, an aging trailer being pulled behind it, and his face turned puce.

"This? This is who you are travelling with for four months, when you should be preparing for your future? This is what you are throwing away your success on? I'll see him charged with abduction!"

I sighed, and let the anger that I hadn't known I possessed flow out of me in one heaved breath. "But think of the scandal. What would the Partners think of you if they knew your crazy wayward daughter became a carnie? That would never do. Best to let sleeping dogs lie. Maybe you should tell them I'm dead instead?" I spat the words like a river of acid between us.

I rolled my bag down the driveway and Dallas got out of the car to meet me. He stepped toward my father, his hand outstretched. "Mr. Jefferson, I'm Dallas Hellson…" My father turned from him as if he were invisible.

"I refuse to let you throw away everything your mother and I have worked so hard for, on some hillbilly circus." He grabbed my arm and yanked me back towards the house. I tripped forward, barely catching my footing and gaped. Not only because this was the first time my father had ever laid a hand on me in anger, but because this was the first time he'd ever touched me at all. He'd never given me so much as a pat on the back or picked me up when I'd fallen.

I was so shocked by it, I just planted my feet and stared, only mildly aware that his grip was so tight that it was bruising the soft flesh of my upper arm.

Dallas stepped forward, putting an arm around my shoulders, a gentle show of support, and placed his other huge hand on my father's chest.

"Sir, you need to let go of Olivia. You are hurting her." His voice was calm but hard. There was an undertone of controlled violence in its depths.

Dallas was young, I'd put his age in his early twenties, but he was tall and well-built from hours of manual labor. My father, by contrast, was sixty years old, short and had a rapidly softening waistline that he hid behind expensive suits.

My father wisely let go.

His arm still wrapped around my shoulders, Dallas picked up my bag and took it to the pickup, placing it in the back next to a battered toolbox. Opening the door for me, he held my elbow as I hoisted myself into the truck.

I turned one last time, but my father had already gone into the house. My mother remained on the porch.

"Goodbye, Mother."

She just sniffed, shook her head in disgust, and returned to the house.

I settled into the passenger seat, and Dallas closed the door with a soft thud. He climbed into the driver's seat, but didn't turn over the ignition.

"Have you changed your mind? I can take you anywhere you need to go." His voice was rough, but his words were gentle.

"No, I haven't changed my mind. Just go," I whispered. He nodded and pulled away from the curb.

Then I burst into tears.

· · ·

DALLAS LET me cry myself out, remaining silent except for the occasional reassuring pat on my arm. My tears drying on my cheeks, I turned toward the window, embarrassed that Dallas had witnessed my meltdown. I watched the long, straight line on the side of the highway, until my eyes were heavy and I fell asleep.

I was awoken by a gentle hand shaking my shoulder, and the midday sun was already high in the sky.

"Olivia, we're here." Dallas's voice was soft, and kind of hesitant, like he was trying to wake a bear. Or worse, a toddler.

"Call me Livvy," I mumbled on a yawn, my mouth cottony from sleep.

"Well, Livvy, guess what? You snore," Dallas laughed, looking in the rearview mirror as he reversed the little trailer beside a much larger one with practiced ease. He jumped out of the truck's cab and came around to open my door.

I could hear Angela's voice in my head. *Well,* she would have said, *unlike me, chivalry isn't dead after all.* She was always making bad taste jokes like that, trying to make us laugh towards the end.

I slid from the truck, which felt a million miles from the ground, and Dallas hovered to make sure I didn't fall flat on my face.

"Leave your bags. I'll take you over to the chow

tent to meet everyone before someone kicks the hive and this place looks like a madhouse." I followed him to where a small crowd of people milled around a large, khaki tent. Dallas's hand rested over my lower back, propelling me towards my fate while giving me the after-school special on carnivals.

"Every year we get some seasonal workers, mostly kids who've just left school and want to see a little of the South, or LA, before college starts in the fall, but don't have enough money to do it alone. Travelling with the carnival is a good way to set yourself up for the year ahead. We don't pay too badly, you get a tent and all your meals are free. But Ruben will explain all that when you sign the paperwork.

"Anyways, we have a few who come back year after year. Some even worked here when my Dad ran the place." A flicker of sadness ran across his face, but his usual smiling countenance returned almost immediately. "And the rest of the people are family."

We'd finally reached the crowd and Dallas maneuvered me into the fray. A tall man in his late forties, with a weathered face and salt and pepper hair, slapped Dallas on the back. "'Bout time you got here, son. Find yourself a hitchhiker?"

"Nah, this is Livvy, she'll be working the ducks

over summer while Liz recuperates." The man's face grew somber, and he slid a look to the other side of the tent, toward a young woman with a baby capsule balanced at her feet. That must be the infamous Liz. Apart from a sour look on her face, she looked healthy enough.

The man looked back at me. "Well, welcome to Hellson Brothers, Livvy. I'm Wyatt; I'm Dallas's cousin. And that beautiful woman over there is my wife, Elise." He pointed to a woman around the same age as him, perhaps a little younger, in a long, white cotton dress, a large smile lighting up her face. She was serving food behind a trestle table, joking with the man in front of her. I smiled and turned back to Wyatt, who was looking at his wife with that goofy expression that shouted *LOVE*. I shook Wyatt's proffered hand.

"Nice to meet you," I squeaked out over the noise.

"I'm just going to introduce her to Rube," Dallas said, leading me through the crowd, stopping occasionally when someone spoke to him, and introducing me every time. There was no way I was going to remember all these names. I worried my lip with my teeth until I could feel it begin to swell. I had to stop or I would look like I'd had Botox injections.

Finally, we reached the other group. Liz stood talking to Wyatt's wife, Elise, who had joined them.

There was an older woman behind the trestle table now; she seemed to be wearing so many strings of beads that she had a slight hunch.

Another woman stood beside Elise, in her late sixties, with tight grey curls and Dallas's clear blue eyes. Definitely a relation; perhaps his mother?

However, towering over the rest of the group was the biggest man I had ever seen. He was easily six and a half feet tall, probably more, but it was the impressive width of his shoulders that made him look so dominating. He had thick, muscular arms, probably from working the carnival. He looked like a bodybuilder, without the bad tan and the mankini.

"Rube, this is Olivia Jefferson, the new sideshow hand I was telling you about. Livvy, this is my brother Ruben, my sister Liz, and my aunts Ida and Elise."

I murmured some kind of response to their polite greetings, and felt distinctly uncomfortable under the piercing gaze of Ruben. He had the same clear blue eyes as Dallas, obviously a family trait, but his seemed to take in everything at once; my wrinkled clothes, my hair that stood up at odd angles from the truck's leather seats, the twitchy movements I made with my hands when I was nervous and the way I was gnawing at my lip like a possessed toddler. His gaze lingered on my puffy eyes, his brows lowering as he shot a questioning look to Dallas, who shrugged.

He turned back to me. "Welcome to the carnival, Olivia." I let out a relieved breath. I felt as if I'd passed some kind of test.

"Thanks," I said, and Dallas started talking to his Aunt, giving me time to take in the group.

Other than the eyes, and maybe the shape of his nose, Ruben didn't look much like Dallas at all. In fact, he looked far more like Liz than Dallas. They both had high foreheads and sharp cheekbones that hinted at some form of Native American heritage, and thick, dark mahogany hair. Liz was also tall for a teenage girl, creeping up towards six feet, and towering over my own humble 5'5. She was reed thin, though I could still see the slight pouch of cushioning from her pregnancy.

I looked away from Liz's scowling face and into Ruben's stern one, and unease stirred in my gut. Maybe I was being rash. I didn't know these people, or how they lived. This was a mistake.

Before I had a chance to say anything, the baby at Liz's feet let out a small mewling cry. Everyone turned towards the baby carrier on the ground. Then they looked at Liz. She stared at them all with defiant dark eyes, before turning and leaving the tent, the baby carrier still on the ground where she left it, and the irate baby still tucked safely inside.

Ruben's brow knitted, and he let out a frustrated sigh. He bent and scooped the tiny infant out of its carrier, the baby comically small in his huge hands.

"I'll go get her a bottle," Ida suggested, moving towards a large white trailer.

Ruben looked down at the baby and his face, which had been all hard lines and stone cold stoicism a moment before, suddenly softened. It actually reminded me of that science experiment you did in grade school with the cornstarch and water. When you squeezed, it was hard and edgy, but as soon as you relieved the pressure, it softened until it melted through your fingers like water.

Settling the baby in the crook of one massive arm, he gazed down at the still fussy baby with bare-faced love.

"What's her name?" I asked, knowing it was a girl as she was clothed from head to toe in cotton candy pink.

Ruben's eyes dragged away from the baby. "Iris," he replied, his face losing its softness, morphing back to the neutrality of business. "I have your contract in my truck. But first, I need you to under-stand that this isn't a holiday. You'll be expected to work hard. The pay isn't great, but meals and board are included. So if you came here expecting some kind of Sweet Valley Summer fling with Goldilocks over there," he tilted his head towards a blushing Dallas, "then you may as well turn around and go home now."

I let a little sputter of useless air out of my gaping mouth, momentarily mute.

"Jesus, Rube. It's not like that." Dallas's cheeks were still tinged pink. Ruben gave Dallas a stern look, and suddenly the age gap between them seemed larger than it was. He seemed more like a father than an older brother, despite there being only half a dozen or so years between them at the most, by my calculations

My previous uncertainties came back, and I toyed with the idea of going home. But then I remembered my father, and the confrontation, and my promise to Angela. I straightened my spine.

"I can work hard, Sir. I'll pull my weight."

He gave me a nod and a small smile. "Ruben will do. Not Sir."

Ida returned with the bottle. I expected him to hand the baby to one of the older women, but instead he took the bottle from Ida with a gentle thank you and placed the teat to the baby's lips. She latched onto it like a piranha and I let out a little snort of laughter.

"Let's go sign your paperwork. Dallas, get to work. I'm sure Olivia doesn't need you to hold her hand the entire summer." I laughed, although the idea was appealing.

Dallas gave Ruben a jaunty salute. "Yessir!" he mocked, and gave me a quick wink as everyone dispersed towards the big rigs. I could see now what he'd meant about "kicking the hive". With lunch over, people milled about everywhere, carrying, lifting, hammering, unhitching and a whole bunch of other activities that made the campsite buzz.

Ruben started off toward the other side of the field, the baby still cradled against his chest. If there was a safer child in the world at that moment, I didn't think it existed outside the animal kingdom. Ruben looked like he would happily tear off heads to protect the six pound human in his arms.

"How much has Dallas filled you in on?" He asked as we reached a late model pickup, shining black in the Florida sun. Unlike Dallas's truck, it had a back seat, with a baby capsule and a whole bunch of archive boxes and papers. He placed the baby in the capsule gently, but the baby didn't fuss, just continued to pull from the bottle, her little face solemn.

"Uh, he hasn't told me much. Just that you needed someone because Liz was recovering from the birth of the baby." Although Liz had looked healthy enough to me. I'd pinned her age around my own, maybe a little younger. My parents would have been horrified if I'd come home pregnant. I shuddered to even think about it.

Ruben raised his eyebrows, searching through one of the cardboard boxes. "That's one way to put it, I guess. Liz suffers from postpartum depression. She's had a rough time. She hasn't bonded with Iris, she rarely gets out of bed unless we are moving sites. The doctors have referred her to a psych, but she refuses to go." He let out a frustrated sigh, and looked... bewildered.

"Anyway, she's moved in with Ida to ensure she has help with Iris during the night, so her trailer is sitting empty. It's yours for the summer. Pay is a flat rate of a seventy-five bucks a day, including food. You'll be manning the lucky ducks and the clowns at smaller carnivals, or one or the other at the larger venues. If your booth makes over a base quota, you get a bonus of ten percent of the extra. Any questions?"

"Where's Iris's father?" The question just slipped out, and I slapped a hand over my mouth.

Ruben frowned. "Conveniently disappeared six months into Liz's pregnancy." Stormy violence

29

settled on his face at the thought. "Any other questions about the *job*?"

I shook my head vigorously, deciding it was better to keep my mouth shut. He thrust two forms in front of me.

"Good. These are the standard employment contracts. Fill them in and sign them. Don't forget the section with your social security number. Hellson Brothers runs on the up and up, unlike some of the other shows out there."

I put pen to paper and signed my life away, as Ruben picked up the baby, and placed her on his shoulder, patting her back gently with his giant mitt of a hand. As I was signing the bottom of the first page, the baby let out a belch worthy of a college frat boy.

I laughed, and the baby smiled, as did Ruben. He signed the bottom of the forms with his freehand, and it was done.

"Welcome aboard. I look forward to working with you over the summer. Now go find Dallas and get to work." His eyes were sparkling with mirth, and his lips curled at the edges, and a part of me relaxed. I gave him a quick grin and did what I was told before either of us had a chance to change our minds.

CHAPTER THREE

"Please ma'am, I'm going to have to insist you get your son out of the water," I said for the fourth time. The woman pretended not to hear me as she whined to her friend that Jerry (her husband I assumed) was spending all his free time away from work with his best friend Mike, even lying about where he'd been, because she'd seen his car parked out the front of Mike's place. She thought that Jerry and Mike were going out and picking up women. I had a sneaking suspicion that his wife's nasal whining had driven Jerry into the arms of Mike himself. It would be totally understandable.

I reached in and plucked the four year old from the water, depositing him beside his mother. Of course, the kid promptly began to cry.

The woman whipped around to face me. "Did

you just touch my son?" Her already nasal voice rose another octave, outrage flushing her cheeks an unattractive shade of red.

"I apologize ma'am, but as I said several times, children are not allowed to sit in the water. This is a carnival, not a water park." I winced at my own tone, but this lady had been the last in a long line of assholes who'd visited my booth since we'd opened this morning. Every second person yelled at me because their kid didn't get a high enough total for the big prize that they wanted, plus two teenagers stole a duck and I'd had to chase them down until Ruben had collared them and they'd given the duck back under his menacing stare.

He'd walked me back to the sideshow, and gruffly told me never to leave the booth unmanned, before striding off into the crowd again. And as if that weren't enough for one day, Liz had been giving me the stink eye all day, rousing herself from her bed long enough to cut me scathing looks and mumble snide remarks to her friends. The benevolent part of me was glad she was up and around. The not-so-nice side of me felt like flipping her the bird.

Currently, the irate mother had turned on me like a savage beast. "Listen here you little inbred bitch, I wa-"

"Sorry ladies, is there a problem?" Dallas

appeared from nowhere and gave us a brilliant smile. Angela would have called it a panty-dropping smile.

"This *employee*," she emphasized the word, "has been extremely rude to me, and she touched my child without my permission." I ground my back molars, but held my tongue.

Dallas nodded sympathetically. "I see. I do apologize, ma'am. She just got out of the institution, and she's having a hard time adjusting to life on the outside of a padded room," Dallas said, completely deadpan. "We just wanted to help her reintegrate back into society."

I kept my face neutral. "The voices tell me to burn things," I said in an eerie monotone.

The woman blanched and grabbed her son's hand, hurrying off in the direction of the gate.

I smirked and rolled my eyes at Dallas. "Really? The institution?"

Dallas burst out laughing, deep chuckles making his shoulders shake. "You do creepy pyro suspiciously well." I ducked my head so he wouldn't see me blush at his words. I was pretty sure that was the nicest compliment I'd ever gotten from a guy. Considering the only other compliment I'd ever received was from Paul in the mathletics club, who said he hoped one day we could subtract our clothes and multiply, it wasn't much of a feat.

He continued to chuckle as he helped me stow my booth for the night. The carnival was starting to wind down in the darkness. The moon was bright in the clear night sky. The dew was starting to fall, making the grass slick beneath our feet, and the fur of the stuffed prizes was beginning to dampen.

I was exhausted. Set up the day before last had been hours of hard labor, and the muscles of my arms and legs still ached. When Dallas had finally shown me where I would live for the next four months, I'd fallen face first onto the bed and gone straight to sleep before the door had even shut behind Dallas's departing back.

Then I'd been trained in how everything worked yesterday, my brain filled to maximum capacity with procedures and numbers. On top of all that, most people had treated me like scum all day. Now, I was just bone tired, both physically and mentally. I didn't know how the other workers did it, year after year.

Everything stowed away for the night, we took my money belt to Aunt Ida's office, where she would count today's takings, put the float back in my belt and stow the whole lot in the safe inside Dallas and Ruben's trailer. When that was completed, Dallas escorted me to the food tent for supper.

The old lady with the mass of beaded necklaces and the slight stoop was the head cook. Her name was Baba, and when Dallas had introduced me, she'd wrapped me in her bony arms and hugged me like a long lost relative.

"Anything you need, you come see Baba," she'd said in heavily accented English, pinching my cheek before she'd waddled off back to the kitchen. I'd learned that she was married to Ted, the old guy who operated the Hurricane.

Dolly, who ran the food van, helped serve behind the long tables, ladling some kind of thick stew filled with meat, veggies and aromatic herbs into disposable bowls or people's private mess kits. The smell wafted into the night air through the gauze of the tent. They easily fed ninety people every day.

The carnival ran like a small city, tents filling the available spaces between the vans, although I shuddered at the thought of being stuck in a tent for four months. Portable toilet and bathroom facilities were hitched to the back of someone's truck and moved from site to site, although if the city grounds where the carnival operated had facilities, we used those too. Luckily for me, Dallas had parked my small van next to his and Ruben's fancy double wide, and he'd insisted I use their bathroom any time I liked. I was secretly glad. Though when I'd ran into Ruben yesterday morning coming out of the shower with only a towel wrapped around his narrow waist, I'd almost been floored. The guy was built like a statue. A really buff statue with abs like a washboard.

He'd given me an assessing look as I'd mumbled about Dallas and the bathrooms, looking anywhere but back at his body. He'd just grunted a good morning and walked into his room, shutting the concertina door. He hadn't said anything about it today, so I was secretly hopeful my bathroom privileges hadn't been revoked.

Baba spooned a huge helping of stew into my deep plastic bowl, and handed me two biscuits instead of one with a conspiratorial wink. I gave her a grateful smile. I'd never had grandparents, both sets had died more than a decade before I was born, so I found myself preening under Baba's affection.

I walked over to the empty spot beside Dallas, who sat at a table full of people, including the friendly faces of Wyatt and Elise, and the not so friendly snarl of Liz on the end of the bench seat. I walked carefully, my eyes on my bowl of soup, trying hard not to slosh the hot liquid over the brim and onto my hands. Amateur mistake.

Liz thrust out a foot, tangling it in mine and I pitched forward, soup flying out in a wide arc and biscuits falling to the ground like lead. I dropped my bowl to catch myself, and landed on my hands and knees in soup.

Dallas was on his feet and around the end of the table immediately, helping me to my feet.

"Are you okay?"

I could feel every set of eyes in the room focused on me. "I'm fine," I mumbled, wiping grass and dirt off my palms.

Liz let out a mean laugh. "This is who you replaced me with? This klutz in designer jeans? What does this silver spoon, trust fund princess know about our life? Nothing. She won't last a week. I just hope she doesn't destroy the place on her way out," she said loudly, ensuring that everyone in the tent could hear.

"Elizabeth, that's enough!" Wyatt's voice was firm.

Dallas picked up my bowl. "I'll go get you some more. I promise not to drop it," he joked awkwardly, but I stepped away.

"Uh, no. It's fine. I'm not hungry anyway. I'm just going to go to bed," I said, backing out of the tent. Baba said something as I walked past, but I couldn't hear her over the roar of embarrassment in my ears.

As soon as I was out of the tent, I ran towards my trailer. I could hear Dallas shouting my name, but I didn't stop. I ran past a confused Ruben, but didn't meet his eyes. I ran until I reached my door, wrenching it open and launching myself at the bed, burying my face in the soft grey comforter.

I didn't cry. Despite my mini meltdown the other day, I wasn't a big crier. I punched my pillow and called Liz every curse word in my vocabulary. Anger churned in my gut, until my empty stomach felt raw with it. I took a breath, and did the deep breathing exercises that I learned when Angela was sick.

Someone had suggested that Angela go to meditation to help control the pain. Ange had insisted I come too. Despite the anger, the memory made me smile.

Adnan Roshi was an actor. Lithe and good-looking in an oriental kind of way, he had a deep voice that belied his short stature and fine bones. He ran a guided meditation class out of his two room apartment, in a complex on 31st street.

On the first day, Angela and I, both dressed in yoga pants and oversized t-shirts, had stood in the hall outside his apartment, the smell of incense leaking from the gap under the door. Several other women waited with us, mostly in their early forties.

Angela had her head wrapped in a bright colored turban scarf. The chemo had made her hair patchy and lank, until she'd just shaved it off. I'd be damned if it didn't make her just look adorably elfin. But she still had the dark smudges beneath her eyes, and her skin was nearly translucent from spending all her summer in a hospital bed.

If you didn't know her, you'd be fooled by her bright smile that showed a mouth full of orthodontically perfect teeth. But I did know her, and I could see a tightness around her eyes that told me she was in pain again.

"Do you want some meds? Maybe we'll just go back down to your mom in the car?"

She shook her head. "I'm fine. Really."

Just then, Adnan threw open the door and waved everyone into the apartment theatrically.

"Please enter, but leave your shoes at the door."

Foam yoga mats lined the floor of the living room. Angela and I got two in the back corner, closest to the door. Harp music played lightly in the background, and the strength of the incense in the room burned my nose.

We sat down and waited for everyone to follow suit.

"Please lie on your back," Adnan said, turning towards the iPod dock. He was wearing super tight yoga pants too, and his silhouette gave him a definitive err...outline.

"That's a serious camel tail," Angela whispered.

I sucked back a burst of laughter. "A what?" I whispered back, but Adnan began to speak.

"Relax your body completely. Start with your feet,

consciously relaxing each toe, then the muscles in the arch of your feet. Let your ankles go loose, and your calves..." he spoke in a soft, undulating voice and despite myself and the weirdness of my surroundings, I felt myself begin to relax for the first time in months.

"Now imagine you are in a field, the grass is blowing in the light summer wind. You walk a well-worn path of small yellow flowers to a warm geothermal pool. The water is milky blue and steam drifts from its surface. Next to the pool is a pergola." He rolled his r's, so his pronunciation sounded like purr-gurla. My lips twitched as I held back a smile. I'd been with him completely until that point. I gave myself a stern talking to and closed my eyes again. "You shed your clothes and shoes, as well as your worries, and place them in the purr-gurla.

"You walk away from the purr-gurla..." I felt a slight vibration in the floor and looked over at Angela, who was shaking with laughter, one hand slapped over her mouth, muffling herself. Turning toward me, she mouthed "purrrrrr-gurrrrla" in an exaggerated fashion.

Laughter bubbled up inside me and I pressed my lips together until they hurt. I was huffing deep lungfuls of air violently through my nose, trying to breathe through my silent laughter. But every time I'd look at Angela, who was wheezing like Ernie from Sesame Street, I'd start up again.

"Stop!" I mouthed, and she shook her head, turning

away to take some deep calming breaths, and I did the same.

Finally, we were in control enough to tune back into Adnan.

"The water is parting up over your chest, to your neck, the healing waters cleansing you of your pain..."

The music was making a trickling noise, and as soon as I focused on it, I had to pee. I bumped Angela with my hand and mouthed "I need to pee" when she looked toward me.

"Hold it!" she whispered back and I shook my head. "Hold it," she repeated slightly louder and I started to do Lamaze exercises to keep it in.

"Imagine a great deluge of rain pouring down over your head..." Adnan droned. Great. The music track started to patter with rain and I knew my bladder was going to explode if I didn't go.

I crept up as quietly as I could, tiptoeing out of the room and down the hall. Where would the bathroom be?

I opened the first door, and stood there dumbstruck. It wasn't a bedroom so much as a massive walk in closet. The walls were lined with shelves that held the largest collection of stripper heels I'd ever seen. There were hundreds of pairs; glittery heels, satiny heels, ones covered with rhinestones and sequins, and a pair that looked like Dorothy's shoes from the Wizard of Oz, if Dorothy had been a hooker that is, sitting on a small pedestal in pride of place. *They all glittered under the light of an ornate chandelier.*

I shut the door quickly. So, not that room then. The next door proved to be the bathroom and I went as quickly as possible. I paused outside the shoe room on the way back. I desperately wanted to go in there and try a pair on, but good manners demanded that I pretended I'd never seen the room.

I slipped back into the living area, where everyone was lying completely still, listening to the soft whoosh and tinkle of white noise.

I looked down at Angela and noted that her features had relaxed completely, her shoulders loose. She was in the ease of a deep sleep. I lay back down beside her quietly, careful not to disturb her. I hadn't seen her that relaxed since before her diagnosis.

We went through the last fifteen minutes in total silence, cocooned in the soft music that still managed to block out the street noise. Eventually, Adnan guided us back out, and we all stood, bodies languid and minds temporarily clear of the strain of life.

"First door on the right. I'll keep Mr. Purr-gurla busy," *I whispered and nudged her toward the hall. The great thing about Angela was that she never asked any unnecessary questions, and she slipped silently into the room.*

I chatted to Adnan Roshi about meditation and his acting gigs, and he flirted with me outrageously. I pretended to be flattered, all the while thinking about the small Indian man teetering around on seven inch stripper heels with floating plastic goldfish in the platforms.

Angela reappeared, looking a little shell-shocked, but she graciously thanked Adnan for his time as we walked out the door. We made it all the way to the elevator before she turned to me.

"There's no place like home," she said, deadpan. I snorted out a giggle and we were crying with laughter by the time we got to her mom's car. Despite Adnan Roshi's shoe fetish, or perhaps because of it, we both went back to his apartment twice a week until Angela had gone into hospital for the very last time.

I WAS SHAKEN from my meditation by a knock at the door.

"Livvy, can I come in?"

I didn't really want to see Dallas, but I wasn't rude enough to tell him to go away.

"Sure," I said with a sigh.

He pushed through the door, stooping a little so as to not clip his forehead on the doorframe. He had a plastic bowl and two foil wrapped packages in his hands.

"Baba sent soup and grits and Dolly sent her hazelnut chocolate cake. It's still warm." He placed them on the little dinette table. "Look, I'm sorry about Liz. She can be a bitch, and with the whole Jonas thing, she's gotten real bitter."

I didn't say anything for a moment, instead unwrapping the foil around the cake, eating it first. I needed the chocolate fix.

"Jonas?" I said around a mouth full of cake. Damn, it was amazing.

"Iris' father. She honestly thought he would marry her and they'd be a family. She took it real hard when he just up and disappeared while she slept one night. She hasn't been the same since."

I felt briefly sorry for Liz, but I still thought she was an asshole, so I said nothing. Dallas wasn't finished though.

"I know it's no excuse, and Ruben is going to have a word with her, what good that'll do. Just ignore her, okay?"

I nodded. I'd turn the other cheek for now, but I'd decided that I wouldn't let her get to me. I'd stand up for myself. I wasn't scared little Olivia on her first day of school, getting picked on for years until Angela rescued me. I would hold my ground.

I opened the container of soup that Baba had sent, and it smelled amazing. I wasn't even worried that I would look like a pig in front of Dallas because I was starving. The soup was filled with root vegetables, hot sausage and some kind of thick cut bacon. I soaked my grit in the broth until it lost all structural integrity. Dallas just sat and watched me eat, a small smile on his face.

"So, how was your first solo day?" he asked.

I swallowed a piece of sausage. "It was… interesting." Which was true.

It was never boring, despite the fact that I didn't do anything more mentally taxing than making change. People could definitely sense my nerves, and the mean ones preyed on my visible weakness. But despite all the jerks, of which there were many, there were some good parts too.

Most people were in a jovial spirit, and a lot joked with me about the weather, the duck that someone had drawn eyebrows on that looked distinctly evil, spending too much money in the midway, and that kind of thing. Then there were the kids, and their comical level of concentration as they chose a duck. There were the ones that dove right in and scooped up the duck right in front of them, and then there were the other kind, that zeroed in on their duck and waited until just the right moment to net their elusive bright yellow prey.

Most of the time I handed out minor prizes, plastic tiaras or cheap stuffed bears, but the kids looked like you had just given them pirate's treasure.

Once or twice today a major prize had gone off, and the children had squealed with deafening delight. I told Dallas of the little girl who'd picked the lucky number and had spent ten whole minutes weighing the many benefits of each toy. It had gone something along the lines of "the teddy was pink, and that's my favorite color, but I could ride the brown horsie, but the monkey could give me hugs, but then so could the teddy…" Ten minutes later, she'd settled on a pink and white unicorn so large, that she'd had to hold the head and her dad had to hold its glittery pink tail so its back end didn't drag in the dirt.

Dallas laughed. "That reminds me of a time we were working a little churchyard fete. Two boys, probably about seven or so, pooled their money and bought a lucky ticket." The lucky ticket stand was basically a wall of large stuffed toys, and the spruiker handed out cards with numbers on them, kind of like bingo, but you only had to get one number to win. "Anyway, they ended up getting two lucky numbers on the one ticket. I'd never seen that happen before. They both got the biggest thing on the wall, and I had to strap them to their backs with brown string so they could carry them home." He smiled at the memory, and it made a dimple form in his cheek. I had the sudden urge to dip my tongue into that dimple, but resisted. I watched his mouth as he spoke, mesmerized by the habit he had of wetting his lower lip, and then dragging the full pink flesh between his teeth before he asked a hard question.

We talked for hours. I discovered that he had a secret talent for mimicking the voices of Disney characters. He told me a story about jackknifing his trailer in a laneway, entirely in the voice of Mickey Mouse. The way he told the story was funny enough, but every time he'd say, "Oh Boy!" in that high pitched mouse voice, I'd double over laughing.

Laughing with Dallas completely eradicated any residual anger that I'd clung to, and filled me with more life than I'd felt in years. I crossed my arms on the Formica top of the table, my chin resting on my forearms, and I just watched as he spoke. I must have started to doze, because I briefly stirred as Dallas put a quilt over my shoulders and whispered goodnight.

That was pretty much how my first week at the carnival passed. Fourteen hour days in the sticky heat began to blur together. My hair smelled permanently of deep fried foods and dust, and my body ached in places that I didn't know I had muscles.

In the evenings, after dining in the food tent, Dallas would walk me back to my trailer and we would talk for hours. We talked about our lives, his being more interesting than mine, and I told him all about Angela, and our mutual misadventures, until sleep sucked me under.

There weren't many other girls my age, except Liz, who I had no inclination to befriend. Those who were my age didn't make any overtures of friendship, already happy in their small cliques or friends with Liz, but I didn't really mind. Making new friends felt disloyal to Angela's memory, which I knew was stupid and Angela would be the first person to tell me so, but that was how I felt.

Other than how hard they worked, the other thing that really surprised me about working at the carnival was the prejudice that came from the townspeople. The general consensus seemed to be that all carnival workers were either stupid, criminals or illegal immigrants. Some treated me with barely veiled contempt. Some days I wanted to scream at their prejudicial asses that they were wrong, about me and about the rest of the workers. They were, on the whole, good, hardworking people. I was valedictorian of my class. A lot of the seasonal workers were just looking for an easy way to pay for their college tuition. Ruben had a business degree that hung on his trailer wall. I knew from talking to Wyatt that Aunt Ida was a qualified accountant, and that Wyatt himself was a mechanical engineer. He'd left the carnival when he'd gotten married, and when his daughters had finished college, he and Elise had decided to come back on the road every summer. They had a very nice bungalow in Pasadena.

So despite the prejudices of the townspeople of Madison, Florida, we weren't all unwashed thugs and drug addicts. Hellson Brothers amusements provided for its employees like they were family, and in return they expected a level of professionalism from everyone involved. Taxes were paid, insurance kept up to date and random drug tests were undertaken. If you got done for brawling at a local bar, you were out, no second chances.

From what I could see, Ruben was trying hard to wipe away the stereotype of a carnie, but old biases ran deep, and I found myself biting my tongue a lot in that first week. So I was happy when Sunday rolled around, and the carnival closed its gates to the people of Madison for another year.

My first takedown was something to behold, and it reminded me of a spider taking down its web. It took five men several hours to take down the big rides, each part numbered, checked and rechecked for parts, and secured onto the back of their flatbed trucks. The Hurricane folded up like a parasol, but had to be locked down and secured to its big rig.

The hardest ride, which took double the amount of men and time, was the carousel, with its antique painted ponies and organ music. Aunt Ida, I'd started calling her Aunt Ida because everyone else did, said that the carousel was the first ride in the original Hellson Brothers carnival and amusements, back when her own parents had been alive.

Everyone called the carousel *Lucille* after the Botticelli style nude that the original artist had painted on the column shaft, fine gold lettering proclaiming her *"the world's most beautiful woman, Lucille"*. Between the mirrors on the other edges of the hexagonal shaft were paintings of cherubs and winged horses, but Lucille was by far the most exquisite painting. The carousel was intricate and delicate and took hours and hours to remove piece by painful piece. Watching it was a lesson in efficiency and teamwork. That's not to say there wasn't a lot of cussing and at least one fist fight when someone pulled instead of pushed and gave another worker a gash on his hand. But the anger was over quickly. It was a combination of patience and back breaking labor.

Luckily for me, the midway booths were basically self-contained. The tent was pulled down, the pieces locked in a large metal trunk, and someone came along and hoisted it onto the back of a truck.

I skipped the food tent that night and went

straight to my bed, falling immediately into an exhausted, dreamless sleep.

DALLAS HITCHING my trailer to his truck woke me with a start in the morning. I peeled one eye open, and blearily noted that it was still dark outside. I pulled the covers over my head. Car doors banged and people yelled, and I wrapped the pillow around my head too.

A bang at my door told me I wasn't going to get anymore sleep.

"Rise and shine, Princess. We roll out in ten." Dallas sounded chirpy considering the sun hadn't even made its grand entrance on the day yet.

I dragged myself up and out of bed, wiggling into a semi-clean pair of jeans on the floor. I finger-combed my hair into a high bun and grabbed my toothbrush and toothpaste. The amenities block was already strapped to a truck, so I walked to a tap and brushed my teeth and splashed my face in the frigid water. I wouldn't admit it out loud, but I kinda missed my shower at home, with its three shower heads and great water pressure. I pulled on a hoodie, and slipped Angela's journal into the front pocket. It went with me everywhere, like a security blanket.

I shuffled toward Dallas's truck like a zombie,

barely appreciating the vibrant pinks of the sunrise. I opened the passenger door, and tried to use my abused muscles to pull myself the two feet into the cab. And failed.

I tossed Angela's notebook onto the bucket seat, as if it was its tiny weight and not the twelve corn dogs I'd eaten this week keeping me tethered to the earth. I pushed myself up once more, and two hands grabbed my hips and tossed me into the cab.

"You looked like you needed a hand," Dallas laughed. We'd fallen into a genuine friendship. There was no pressure, and he was perfectly gentlemanly always, treating me like I was a sister. I wasn't sure how I felt about that, as I'd been having some very unsibling-like dreams about him, but I was thankful for his companionship regardless.

He slid into the driver's side and we rolled out of the lot, and then out of Madison City limits.

"So what's up next on that list of yours?" He nodded toward Angela's journal that sat on the seat between us.

"I don't know which to do first."

I actually had no idea how I was going to achieve most of the things on Angela's list. They seemed at least possible when I was at home, with my unlimited credit card and the support of Angela's parents. Now I was out on the road, my parents had cancelled all my credit cards out of spite, which had been an embarrassing experience. Luckily I'd had a couple of hundred dollars squirrelled away, and Ruben had given me an advance on my first paycheck.

There were things on Ange's list that were impossible for me to do in good conscience, even for Angela's memory. Things like "get married by Elvis" and "have three babies". I loved Ange with all my heart, but there was no way I was going to marry some drunk guy in Vegas just to check something of her list

I'd given myself the summer before college to do what I could on that bucket list. I needed that closure before the new chapter of my life began.

"Well, what's the next one? Maybe you can just do them in order?" He reached above the visor, and pulled on a pair of Raybans. The sun had come up, and his skin glowed in the deep golden light. Looking at him made me feel a little breathless.

I cleared my throat and flicked the page. My cheeks flamed and I snapped the book shut.

"What did it say?" he asked. I shook my head, but his hand shot out and he grabbed the journal. He deftly opened it to the right page, his eyes flicking between the road and the journal.

"Fall in love," he read aloud. That wasn't so bad,

even if it was stamped with love hearts. But directly underneath it in bold letters, underlined several times- "And lose my V-Card," Dallas laughed, then laughed harder. "Your friend was wild, that's for sure. Well, that one could be a little difficult. I mean you need time to fall in love, and I don't think you should rush into the second part, unless it's already too late...?"

My face was so red I could have cooked an egg on my cheeks.

"No, I mean I've had boyfriends, I don't think I've been in love, but I've never, you know... I mean..." I snapped my mouth shut to stop the drivel and the little white lie from compounding into a big fat lie. Friends who were boys counted as boyfriends, right?

He held a hand up to stop me. "Say no more, it's none of my business," he cleared his throat. "Okay, how about you just open it to a random page until you find one you can do?"

It was as good an idea as any. I closed the book and opened it toward the back, purposefully away from the offending page.

"It says 'smile and compliment everyone, because you never know if it will be the only beacon in the depths of someone's darkness.'"

I remembered when Angela had written that entry. They'd decided to move her to the palliative care ward. The day after she wrote those words would be one of the worst of my life. Unfortunately, I would always remember it with crystal clear clarity.

THE PERSISTENT BEEPING of Angela's monitors no longer bothered me. They faded into the ambient noise of the hospital ward. The squeak of the nurses rubber soled shoes, the clatter of the food trolley's, the whimpering of the woman one room over as she watched her husband slowly die. It was the nature of the palliative care ward. When Angela was first moved there, it made me so uncomfortable that I stopped visiting for a couple of days. How selfish was that? Angela had been declared terminal and I couldn't deal with the beeping of her monitors. Eventually the self-recrimination had gotten so bad, that I'd returned. Angela hadn't said anything, just looked at me with her big, expressive blue eyes that were full of understanding and acceptance, but had made me feel even guiltier.

Angela took in another rattling breath, and that was louder than anything else in the ward. She was heading downhill fast, and she was so reliant on the morphine drip that she was only with us a couple of hours a day. She opened one eye and looked over at me where I was reading my physics textbook.

"What's..up..nerd?" The cancer had spread to her lungs pretty quickly, and she was essentially gasping for breath every minute of the day. I closed my book and put it beside me.

"Just boring physics. You know, E equals MC squared and all that jazz. How are you feeling?"

Angela smiled at me serenely. "I feel like I'm ready to die, Livvy." Only Angela called me Livvy. My parents didn't like nicknames, but Angela had decided Olivia didn't suit me and had dubbed me Livvy, forevermore.

I reached over and squeezed her hand, my heart feeling like it was being burnt in my chest. "Don't give up, Angie." Tears welled in my eyes as I thought about a world without her. I wasn't ready, and I knew for certain her parents weren't ready, for such a world.

"Don't cry. I'm not going anywhere right now. I wish I could. I'm always in so much pain, Livvy. I don't want you to remember me as this animated corpse," her voice was scratchy and strained. Tears began to stream down my cheeks now. I was selfish, selfish, selfish. I swiped at my cheeks with my sleeve. "I asked the doctor if he could help me. I asked him to kill me."

My mouth swung open. "What did he say?" I squeezed her pale, skeletal hands.

She shook her head. "No, of course. Euthanasia is illegal. But he said, if he could have, he would." With that, Angela's eyelids fluttered and she fell back into her pain filled slumber. Sometimes she'd whimper in her sleep and I felt like I could just shatter on the wind.

Suddenly, I was incredibly angry. I was angry at myself, and at society. Who were we to demand that she spend her remaining weeks of life in agonizing pain? Who were we to dictate when she could die, when every other decision in her life had been hers? Why did this last vestige of dignity have to be denied to her, and in the name of what? Humaneness? There was nothing humane about Angela dying slowly on that hard hospital bed inside these four sterile walls.

I stood quietly and moved out of the room. I walked down the hall and hopped in the elevator. When the doors slid closed and the elevator began to move, I screamed. I screamed out of pain, and out of anger. I screamed at God, and at science, because neither one could save my best friend. The elevator shuddered to a halt and I stepped out, the only testament to my meltdown was a single tear that rolled down my cheek.

I HADN'T REALIZED that I'd been reliving the memory out loud, or that I was silently crying until I felt Dallas pullover, unclip my belt and drag me across the seats into his arms, hugging me tightly against his chest. He stroked my hair and whispered the same soothing nonsense you'd say to a spooked horse.

Once my eyes had stopped gushing water, I pulled away, embarrassed again.

"I swear, I've never cried this much in my life. I'm not normally that girl." I wiped my nose on a wrinkled tissue I pulled from the front pocket of my hoodie.

"Better out than in," he murmured, clipping himself back in and pulling back onto the highway.

I laughed chokingly. "Isn't that a fart?"

"It still applies, though," he smiled.

I silently berated myself for my weakness. I needed to pull my shit together. There was no way I was going to cry my way across eight states.

"I think you need to choose another one as well. You are naturally nice to everyone, so that one isn't even a big leap for you. Do you think there's one in there that says 'Kiss a handsome carnie?'" he teased.

I felt my cheeks redden. "Hopefully not, because I don't think Baba would appreciate me kissing Ted."

Dallas laughed and gave a small shudder, but part of me wondered if he was joking about the kissing thing, or hinting that he wanted to kiss me. Dammit, I missed Angela. I wanted to call her and ask what she thought he'd meant. We'd dissect it, then come up with a twelve step plan to find out if he liked me, of which I would do six steps and then chicken out.

I blew out a sigh and picked up the journal. I flicked to a random page, and prayed it wasn't something outrageous. I let out a whoosh of relief.

Dallas looked over at the journal, and took both hands off the wheel, clapping.

"Ooh girl, you know what this means?" He did his best finger-snap. "Shopping spree and makeover day!"

CHAPTER FOUR

QUITMAN, GEORGIA

I'd been baking under the hair dryer for ten hours. Well, it felt like ten hours but probably wasn't more than one. I always had a problem with forced stillness and I'd been sitting in the salon for about four hours now.

"Okay, Sugar. Let's have a look at this masterpiece, shall we?"

It'd been hard to find a hairstylist in Quitman that could do what I'd asked, but I'd finally tracked one down. She'd taken one look at the picture of what I wanted on Dallas's phone, blinked rapidly, given me a determined smile and then gotten to work.

I didn't think it was supposed to take this long, and I was slightly worried that she'd cooked my hair, and maybe a little of my brain. Part of me was petrified that when she unwrapped my hair, it would all fall to the ground at my feet. I was definitely beginning to feel light headed, but that was probably from the fumes and the fact I hadn't eaten since breakfast.

She wheeled me to a station that had the mirror covered. "I want this to be a wow moment for you, Sugar. So sit back and relax, and we'll do the big reveal with your cute little man buns out there." I turned and realized that Dallas was still waiting on the couch for me. I gave him a little wave, and he waved back, although he'd seemed engrossed in the trashy magazine from 1995, judging by the pop princess on the cover. He laughed at all the foil on my head.

"Protecting yourself from aliens?" He gave me an exaggerated wink, and I flipped him the bird.

Lynette, the stylist, slowly unwrapped each little hair parcel. She made a satisfied mmm each time, which I found reassuring. She got out the handheld dryer, then the curler, then some kind of goop. She flicked and fondled my hair into submission, talking to herself the entire time.

"Perfect, Lynette. You've done it again," she murmured to herself, and I let out a relieved sigh. "Now, Sweetcheeks," she said in an overly loud voice, "I took the liberty of dying you some matching extensions, in case you want some of those gloriously long mermaid locks. I'll put them in now, they just clip in and out." She clipped and pulled, fluffed and brushed, snipping off pieces here and there.

"Okay, we are ready. Sweet buns, come in here and see this," Lynette called to Dallas.

He swaggered in, a huge grin on his face as he stopped beside Lynette.

"Wow. Just wow. A bald spot really suits you, Livvy."

"What!" My hand went to the back of my hair, but there was no bald patches.

Lynette whacked Dallas's arm with a paddle brush. "Bad boy! You should know better than to tease a girl about her hair. Don't worry, Honey. I'll show you right now. Ready? One, two, three!"

She whipped the piece of satin away from the mirror with a flourish and my jaw dropped to my chest. I looked like a mermaid princess. The roots of my hair were a deep royal blue, which gradually get lighter the further down my dead straight hair it travelled until it curled the color of seafoam at the ends. The extensions in my hair were even lighter in color again, a blond that had been lightly tinted a teal color.

It was perfect, like a work of art. I didn't even recognize the girl in the mirror. The blues and greens in my hair made the flat blue color of my eyes sparkle.

"Wow," I breathed, and Lynette clapped her hands together gleefully at my response, her face beaming with pride.

After letting Lynette take a million pictures of her masterpiece, I paid, trying not to wince at the amount. It was almost all my savings, and I was glad the carnival fed me, otherwise I'd be starving for the next week.

Waving goodbye, Dallas took me straight to a tiny little strip mall. It only had three small boutiques; one womens, one mens and one consignment store.

"Let's go there first," I said, pointing to the consignment shop. I needed to watch my budget now.

I pushed through the door and was assaulted by the scent of mothballs.

"We should do this movie montage style," Dallas whispered.

A girl in her early teens was playing on her smartphone behind the counter. "Need help?"

I gave her a warm smile and shook my head. "No thanks, I love your glasses by the way." May as well get a start on my other bucket list item too.

"Thanks," the girl said, not looking back up from

her phone. Well, I guess not everyone was going to appreciate my compliments.

Dallas pulled me to the back of the store. "Here's what we'll do," he stage whispered. He seemed to be enjoying this even more than I was. "You'll grab some things, and I will grab some things, and we'll have a fashion parade with you as the model du jour."

"I didn't know you spoke French!"

"I don't, but I watch a lot of Van Damme movies," he said as he pulled a white cotton dress off the racks.

I shook my head. "I don't think white is your color."

He put the dress against his body and looked down. "All colors are my color, darling."

I'd be damned if he wasn't right; he did look great in white, with his golden tan and blonde hair.

"Maybe I should have been clearer. I'm going to play the devil's advocate and choose stuff out of your comfort zone. You never know, I may be a fashion visionary."

I looked at him in his tight, well-worn Levi's and faded button down plaid shirt. He looked fine, like with a capital F, but I didn't think he was going to be the next fashion guru. Karl Lagerfeld wouldn't lose any sleep over the competition anyway.

Dallas looked so excited that I just nodded, huffed out a sigh and chose six random things from the rack of size tens and walked into the change rooms.

"Nothing that a stripper would wear on the job!" I shouted through the door, and heard him laugh.

The first thing I tried on was a black smock dress that made me look a little like Wednesday Addams. I loved Wednesday, but her look wasn't one I wanted to emulate. I tried on a variety of pastel colored sundresses, and while I liked them, I knew that they would be what the old Olivia would have worn. They were safe, and not really me.

I tried on a blue and white gingham dress in a baby doll cut that had a tight bodice and two little pearl buttons that I undid and showed some cleavage. I looked like the sexy version of Dorothy from the Wizard of Oz, and I thought this outfit would have gone wonderfully with Adnan Roshi's stripper ruby slippers. But the blues of the dress complimented my hair and the cut skimmed my curves flatteringly.

"Okay, give me a look already," Dallas shouted from outside the room.

I walked out and did a self-conscious twirl. He let out a long whistle from between his teeth. "Take me to Wonderland, Alice baby!"

I rolled my eyes, but I could feel myself smiling goofily.

"Alright, my turn. Try this." He thrust a baby blue tea dress into my hands, with a tiny pink flower pattern and a full circle skirt. He handed me a crinoline petticoat as well.

"Have we travelled back to the fifties and I missed the DeLorean?" But a deal was a deal and I took the dress into the change room. It had a low, square cut bodice and was made out of soft satin. I pulled the petticoat up over my thighs and around my hips, and I couldn't fight the childhood urge to twirl around until my skirts flew out. I pulled the dress over my head, getting caught in the lining and skirts.

I tried to swim through all the satin, grunting and muttering.

"What the hell are you doing in there?" Dallas sounded amused from the other side of the door and I growled at him. Finally seeing the light, I pulled the dress down over my hips, which were beginning to border on ample. I'd always been curvy, but Baba's home cooking and my churro addiction were already catching up with me. I sighed. No more churros for me.

I reached around but couldn't zip it even half way up. I opened the door.

"Zip me up?"

Dallas turned, and blinked. Then cleared his throat, leaning around to pull up my zip.

"Damn, Livvy. That's a winner. You look like a wet dream."

I blushed and twirled again, the dress flying up until it touched my fingertips. I had to agree with Dallas, I felt feminine and graceful, neither of which usually applied to my jeans and blouse combo.

"Okay. But it's a bit impractical for everyday wear? I mean, I'm never going to go out, so it'll just sit in my wardrobe-"

"Stop rationalizing and just buy it," Dallas interrupted.

"Okay, okay. So what's next, oh stylist extraordinaire?" He grinned mischievously and disappeared amongst the racks.

An hour, and the rest of my paycheck later, we left the consignment store. Other than the pretty tea dress, I had a couple of long gypsy style skirts that fell right to my toes and made me feel like a flower child. I'd also bought the Dorothy dress, and at Dallas's insistence, a blue velvet bodice top that hooked up at the back and had a pretty scalloped neckline with white lace trim. It hugged me like a second skin, and Dallas's tongue had nearly rolled out of his mouth when I'd tried it on. If the tea dress made me look like beauty and grace, then the velvet bodice made me look like sex and sin. I secretly loved it, but I wasn't sure I'd ever wear it in public.

By the time we pulled back into the lot that was hosting Hellson Brothers for the weekend, it was past dark on our day off. We'd stopped for a pizza at the local diner because we'd well and truly missed the dinner bell.

We pulled into the space between the trailers and sat in the dark for a while. I was not ready to go back to the madness of carnival life just yet.

Today had been everyone's day off, except for Ruben, who had to waltz a bunch of inspectors through the carnival after we'd set up yesterday. For every new state we entered, we had to get inspected. That was on top of the daily safety inspection by the operators and the very frequent spot checks by Wyatt.

So as a result, the carnival employees had flooded the small town of Quitman like a locust plague. Some went to Tallahassee, but most didn't want to spend their day off on the road.

I turned toward Dallas in the darkened cab, and took in his profile as his head rested back against the seat, eyes closed.

"Thanks for today." My voice sounded too loud in the silence.

"S'ok. I had fun," he murmured sleepily.

"Can I ask you something?"

"Boxers, not briefs," he answered and I smacked him lightly on the thigh.

"Not that, dopey. But I'll file it away for later use," I laughed. "I want to know why you are helping me with all this. I know shuffling around after me all day couldn't have been your idea of a relaxing day off."

"I'll have you know that sitting in hair salons reading two decade old tabloid magazines is exactly how I spend my days off."

I whacked him again.

"I'm serious. Why even offer me this job? I'm exactly the green, Park Lane princess that Liz accused me of being. I have no idea what I'm doing most of the time."

Dallas rubbed his leg where I'd whacked him, a faux-hurt look on his face, before that grin lit up his face.

"I don't know, Livvy. I'm a guy, most of the time we don't have reasons to do stuff." I just raised a brow. "Fine. I guess it was because you looked so pathetic on the Hurricane, but you had this stubborn set to your jaw. You looked lost and broken and I could see the sadness in your eyes and it was a look I knew. And for some reason, I just wanted to make you feel better. Then you showed me the list and Angela's photograph and the tragedy of the whole thing just really hit home. I don't know why I wanted to help you, I just knew I had to try."

There was a heavy silence.

"When did your parents die?"

Dallas turned his face away, looking out the driver's side window. No one had come out and said that Ruben, Dallas and Liz's parents were dead, but when they were spoken of, I could tell by the looks on people's faces that they had been well-loved and still missed.

"Six years ago. I was fifteen. It was a stupid accident. The truck rolled and killed them both."

I reached across the gulf of grief between us and held his hand. I didn't say I was sorry, that wouldn't have been enough, but I let him know that I was there. Sometimes when you are lost in grief, the touch of another person was like an anchor.

He squeezed my hand back, and then let go, opening his door and the cool night air rushed in, chasing away the warm safety of the truck. I slid out my own door, pulling all my bags with me.

He walked me to my door, a whole six feet away.

"Well, goodnight," I mumbled. The more time I spent with Dallas, the more attractive I found him.

But he'd made it clear that I was securely in the friend zone.

"Night. Remember, seven A.M. start tomorrow." With that, he was gone.

I threw myself down on my bed and tried not to overanalyze every moment and every action.

I failed.

"Mommy, look, Mommy!" The little girl stomped her foot as her mother tried to wipe the ketchup off the hands, cheeks and strangely enough the eyebrows of her little brother.

"What, Maisy?" the woman snapped. She looked stressed. I'd discovered that after a certain hour, working at the carnival stopped being about having fun and started to be more of a troubleshooter job as harassed parents reached the end of their respective tethers.

"That girl has hair like Ariel's sister. Can I touch it, Mommy?"

"No, Maisy. It's rude to touch other people's hair without permission." The baby was squirming and had somehow managed to spread more ketchup across his face, even though he was finished with his hot dog. His mother held him at arm's length and found an offending cache of sauce on the underside of his sleeve.

I took pity on the woman, who had to start her cleaning procedure all over again.

"It's okay," I said, and squatted down in front of the little girl. The mother gave me a suspicious once over, and then determining I wasn't a threat to her offspring, looked relieved. The little girl reached out and fingered some of my blue tresses.

"Are you actually a mermaid?" Maisy whispered. She was about four or five I'd guess.

I looked around secretively and whispered, "Can you keep a secret?"

A solemn, but vigorous nod.

"I'm really a mermaid princess. I asked the good sea witch for some legs, so I could come on shore and make sure little girls still believed in us. Because if you don't believe, then we can't sing to the waves anymore. And if we don't sing to the waves, everyone out on the boats on the ocean get seasick and then throw up everywhere."

Maisy pondered this for a while, then nodded solemnly. "I'm not allowed on Daddy's boat without my orange jacket. But I've never felt sick."

I gave her a conspiratorial wink. "That's because you believe in mermaids."

Maisy's mom threw me a grateful look. "Come

on, Maisy. Let's go home and give your brother a proper bath. Say goodbye."

"G'bye." I waved as she walked down the midway. The little girl had provided some much needed entertainment during the late afternoon lull.

The carnival was closing down for the night soon, town noise ordinances preventing our usual 9pm close down. I began to stow away the prizes, when I heard a high pitched scream and then yelling. I barreled around the duck pond, and stared down the midway. A crowd had gathered around the Sizzler, a spinning ride where you sat in little pods, secured in by a bar across your lap.

Ruben came barreling around the corner, a baby bjorn strapped across his chest, Iris securely tucked inside. It just looked weird to see such a giant man with a baby carrier on. A hand supporting her head, he stopped in front of my booth.

"Watch the baby," he said, unclipping the carrier and passing Iris to me and dropping the carrier at my feet. "Some idiot stood up on the Sizzler and fell off." He was steamed. He strode off down the midway, the swelling crowd parting for him.

The baby whimpered at being woken up, and I stood there, holding her like she was a porcelain doll that I was sure to break.

She started to yell harder, really working herself

up into a crying jag, so I tucked her to my chest and rocked. I'd never held a baby before, I was working entirely off instinct, and desperately trying to remember what they told us in those useless health classes about holding a baby. I swayed backwards and forwards until her crying subsided into a whimper, and then her whimpers were merely sleepy snuffles. By that time though, my arm was dead. Babies might be small, but if you hold them long enough, they began to feel like lead weights.

An ambulance made its way down the lane between the midway booths, followed by the police, and I knew it was going to be a long night for Ruben. I wondered where Liz was so I could give her back her baby.

Emmanuel, two booths up, was finishing up the pack up on his booth, though his gaze kept straying up the midway like everyone else.

"Manny, can you just watch my booth for a sec? I need to find someone else to watch Iris."

"No worries," he shouted down to me, and I headed towards the food tent, down behind the vans. Hopefully Baba or Aunt Ida would be there somewhere.

Unfortunately, the place was deserted except for Wyatt, who was pacing around muttering about "damn stupid teenage boys," with the phone to his ear. He turned and saw me, smiling tightly in my direction.

"Sorry, Olivia. That kid has created a mountain of paperwork. I'm just on hold. I mean, thank the lord the kid is fine, just a broken arm apparently. But he's in a lot of pain. Hope it was worth it to impress the girls in the car behind him. Getting hit by the arm of the Sizzler is no fun, I can tell you that one from experience. He's lucky not to be dead."

"Have you seen Liz? Or even Baba or Ida? Someone to look after Iris?"

He shook his head. "Ida took Liz to her post-natal appointment in Tallahassee. Elise is the first aid officer so she'll be over by the Sizzler. I haven't seen...Yes? Hello, this is Wyatt Hellson of Hellson Brothers Amusements, policy number..." he said when someone came back on line on his phone.

I walked back to my booth and found Manny had stowed everything and cleaned it.

"Still babysitting? Don't worry about it, Olivia," I loved the way Manny said my name with his heavy Spanish accent. He really drew out the vowels, and made it sound very exotic. "You go put the bambina down. I've got this covered."

"Thanks, Manny. I owe you one."

With no better ideas, I took Iris back to my trailer. Gently maneuvering the door open, I walked to the bed and laid the baby down, holding my breath, hoping she didn't wake. I walked back to the door and propped it open, letting in the cool evening breeze. I turned on the little desk fan to move the stagnant air.

I checked on the baby, who hadn't stirred, so I double checked she was still breathing. Staring intently at the rise and fall of her tiny chest, I propped pillows along the edge of the bed so she couldn't roll off, but far enough away that she wouldn't roll into the pillows and suffocate. I grabbed a soda from the small fridge and sat down to watch the baby, just in case she decided to jump up and poke a finger in the electrical socket or something.

The hubbub of the carnival died down, and the only people left were employees and the cops. Everyone would be questioned, and the cops and officials would decide if we would open tomorrow or not.

I opened my copy of *A Picture of Dorian Gray* and settled into my role as babysitter.

About an hour later, my door was wrenched open, startling me out of my trance.

"What is your problem, bitch? Is stealing my job, my trailer and my brothers not enough for you? You have to steal my kid too?" She strode over to the bed and yanked the baby into her arms hard enough that it made me wince and leap to my feet. Iris began to scream.

"Its okay, Mommy's here," Liz crooned, as if she wasn't the one that just hurt her in the first place. Liz had a death grip on the infant, whose face was turning an angry shade of red.

"I think you are holding her too tight," I said quietly, but Liz looked at me like a rabid wolf.

"Don't tell me how to hold my own baby, Princess. I'll hold her however I want."

Iris was really howling now, and I contemplated beating Liz over the head with the lamp and taking my chances at catching the baby. Liz was out of her mind. My hand moved to the lamp, when the door banged open again.

"Elizabeth!" A voice boomed from the doorway.

Liz immediately loosened her grip on the baby.

Ruben stood in the doorway, his face like thunder. "Here, take that stupid brat. I know she's all you want anyway, you don't give a fuck about me. If it wasn't for it, Jonas would still be here and my life wouldn't be ruined." Liz thrust the baby roughly into Ruben's arms as she pushed past him and out the door.

Ruben made hushing noises, but the baby was scared and hungry.

"I'm sorry," I said over the sound of Iris' cries.

Ruben shook his head. "Not your fault." He held the baby gently against his chest and walked towards his trailer.

I slumped back down on the bench seat and let out a ragged breath. My hands were shaking. The look on Liz's face had chilled me. In that moment of rage, I wasn't so sure she wouldn't have hurt Iris.

THE NEXT DAY, Liz was gone. Disappeared from the carnival with all her bags, but without Iris. She left a note for Ruben, telling him not to look for her, or so Dallas said.

Of course, the first thing they did was look for her. They called all the family, even Jonas, but no one had heard from her. They searched all over town, showing her picture at the bus station, but she was gone without a trace.

Ruben filed a missing person's report, but the cops weren't overly worried and it got placed at the bottom of their in-trays.

The carnival was closed for the day while yester-day's Sizzler accident was investigated, but they hoped to open again on Sunday.

It was then I discovered that there was nothing sadder than a deserted carnival. Most people were out looking for Liz, or picking up supplies so they could hit the road on Monday. I wandered between the rides, and around the booths, a little aimless without Dallas or the crowds of people.

Eventually, I made my way to see Baba. The smell of the food tent was heavenly.

Baba was watching Iris and preparing dinner. "It smells wonderful in here. You are such an amazing cook."

The old polish woman smiled, and the deep crinkles by her eyes spread out towards her greying temples.

"Thank you, *Myszko*. Come here and peel the potatoes while I feed the little *dzidzia*." She said, indicating the gurgling Iris. She pulled a bottle from where it was heating in the bottle warmer.

I was getting used to Baba's strange mix of polish and English. I knew *myszko* meant mouse, because I'd asked, and by the process of elimination, I deduced that *dzidzia* meant baby, or something like that. I sat down in a chair across from the wooden trestle table and began peeling a huge bag of potatoes. As far as I could tell, Baba was the only person in the company who cooked, other than Dolly, who spent all day in the food van anyway. That made Baba the most appreciated person in the whole company.

"What's on your mind, little one?" she asked, placing the bottle into Iris's gaping mouth.

"Nothing."

Baba raised both eyebrows at me disbelievingly.

"I kind of feel like this whole thing with Liz is my fault."

She made a dismissive noise in her throat. "*Nie,* the problems with Liz started well before you arrived. She was only eleven when Thomas and Jenny were killed, may they rest in peace." She crossed herself. "It hit her hard; she was their baby. She changed from a sweet little girl into a troubled teen almost overnight. We all let her get away with too much, feeling sorry for her. A girl without a mother is a terrible thing, despite Elise and Ida doing their best. Then she got pregnant to that no good Jonas, and she has been acting out ever since. Do not lay the blame for this at your own feet, *Myszko.*"

The baby was asleep, and Baba removed the bottle from her mouth and picked up a potato, peeling it with a well-practiced speed that would have had me chopping off a finger if I'd tried to keep up.

We sat in peaceful silence for a moment, no noise but Iris's breaths and the scrape of knives.

"What will happen to Iris if Liz doesn't come

back?" I whispered, doing my best not to wake the baby.

"Ruben, he is listed as a guardian for the baby. He and Liz decided it was for the best when it became obvious that that good for nothing donkey was not coming back." She made a spitting motion towards the grass, and I wrinkled my nose. Baba dropped her voice. "That Ruben, he is not as tough as he looks, all hard face. Inside, he is soft. Like all good men. Like your Dallas."

"He's not *my* Dallas," I protested and Baba just rolled her eyes.

"But you like him, no?"

"Yes, I mean no. We are just friends." I felt the blush creep up my neck, my ears and cheeks burning. The old lady cackled.

"Okay, *Myszko.* Whatever you say. Now chop the carrots, people will be hungry!"

THE FOOD TENT was eerily quiet over dinner. While they hadn't had any luck finding Liz, the safety inspector had passed the ride and the carnival was cleared to open for the final day on Sunday, or so Wyatt told me. Dallas and Ruben were still out looking for Liz.

Eventually, Aunt Ida came to take Iris home to

her bassinet, and her face looked pinched with worry. The tightness to everyone's expressions broadcasted the worst case scenarios. What if Liz had done something really dumb and hopped in a car with a serial killer? Or worse, taken her own life? It weighed heavy on my conscience, despite Baba's reassurances that it wasn't my fault.

I sat outside my trailer on a folding chair, waiting for Dallas to return, trying not to imagine the worst case scenario. Eventually his truck pulled in, and he shuffled over to me, worry and exhaustion etched on his face.

I leapt to my feet. "Any news?"

"A guy at the bar saw a girl fitting Liz's description hitching her way out of town on the northbound lane last night. We don't know where she's going, we can only hope she gets there safely." He looked shattered. He shuffled toward the trailer he shared with Ruben, oddly two dimensional.

I watched him go with an odd sense of regret and relief.

We reopened the carnival again on Sunday, the last day of our stay in Quitman. It was predictably quiet, given the accident on the Sizzler and the subsequent local press. Even though it was the kids own fault, public opinion had swayed, and we were no longer welcomed into local businesses, and hardly anyone but the odd group of teenagers came through the gates.

Ruben looked beaten down. Black smudges swept under his eyes, and he looked a decade older. Tear down began, and his face grew stormier and stormier. I could see his worry curling into anger, and I decided to stay well out of his way.

Liz's friends all gave me dirty looks and snide comments, picking up where Liz had left off. I wanted to scream at them that it wasn't my fault, but I wasn't so sure that that was true. Plus, a small secret part of me was glad she was gone.

CHAPTER FIVE

CAIRO, GEORGIA

Carnival life went on, despite Liz's rapid departure and the debacle of Quitman. Too many people relied on the living provided by the carnival, so everyone was extra friendly, spruiked harder and encouraged people to visit the midway in order to recoup the losses of the last stop. Dallas spent more time with me after the carnival closed for the night, not wanting to spend too much time alone.

Iris seemed to spend more time with me, too. With Liz gone, she shifted between babysitters, usually Baba or Elise during the day, and Ruben, Dallas or Aunt Ida of a night. Usually when Dallas came to visit me in my Airstream, Iris came too. I didn't mind. Once I got past the initial awkwardness of holding a baby, I found her tiny baby antics amusing. She was a quiet and solemn baby, but she passed wind like a pony.

All the baby stuff had been moved to the guy's trailer, and it suddenly was covered in baby blankets and assorted baby paraphernalia.

"You haven't picked another bucket list item," he said on our second night in Cairo, his high Mickey Mouse voice amusing Iris as he tickled her ribs, making her gurgle.

I sat across from them at the dinette, writing in the journal, documenting my grand adventure. "I don't have to do one every week. Besides, I did two last week." Between us was a large pepperoni pizza, and I put down my pen to eat a slice.

"I'll choose one for you," he said, reaching over to the table to pick up Angela's journal, flicking slowly through the first couple of pages.

He stopped and smiled at one page, showing it to the baby.

"Look, it's Livvy," he cooed in a high pitched baby voice. "This is a cool picture. It looks like you had fun."

I leaned toward him, looking at what he was talking about. It was a picture of Angela and me, our arms wrapped around each other, standing on a bar, singing into our sodas and dancing. You could see the back of the security guy's head as he demanded we get down. I laughed. I loved that picture too. Someone had seen me taking Ange's picture, and insisted I get up there too, snapping dozens of pictures of our little foray into tabletop dancing.

"What were you singing?" Dallas asked, continuing to flick the pages.

"*We Built This City* by Starship." I smiled at the memory. We'd both been completely tone deaf, but the people in the bar had applauded us anyway, as we were dragged off the bar and out the door.

"We built this city! We built this city on rock-'n'roll..." Dallas sang off-key and I winced, but Iris cooed along happily.

"Iris likes my singing, don't you, Sugar?"

He paused on a page, and a slow smile that I did not completely trust spread across his face. He snapped the journal shut and handed it back to me.

"I'm dropping Iris back to Ruben, then we are going for a drive. Dress warm. And in black. You have five minutes."

"What?" I asked, but the door was already banging behind him.

True to his word, he reappeared in minutes, dressed in tight black jeans that did amazing things for his thighs and a black hoodie. I'd thrown on my black sweater and my yoga pants quickly. The combination didn't really go, but there wasn't a lot of black in my wardrobe.

He hustled me into his truck and we drove through the streets of Cairo, and out into residential area.

Every time I asked where we were going, he'd raise a hand and tell me to "just wait."

We drove out of the densely populated areas, into the streets right on the outskirts, where there were no street lights.

"Are you finally going to murder me?"

Without answering, he pulled over to the side of the road. Jumping out, he climbed onto the back of his pickup and rustled around in the big lockbox that was bolted to the tray.

"Are you looking for a hacksaw? Should I run?" I yelled through the glass partition.

He looked up and shook his head. "Seriously, Liv. If I was a murderer, I wouldn't tell you if you should run or not. Have you never watched a horror movie? Ah ha!" He pulled a large spanner out of the toolbox.

"Okay, get out of the truck."

"No!"

"I'm not going to murder you, for fuck sake!"

"That's what they all say," I grumbled, but got out of the truck and looked around.

It looked like the rural outskirts of any town.

Houses were sparse, trees were plentiful and it was very, very dark. "Okay, if you aren't about to go all Jack the Ripper on me, what the hell are we doing out here in the middle of nowhere?"

He pointed to the street sign with his spanner. Angela Ave.

"Bucket list item number seven: break the rules. We, and by we I mean you, are going to steal this street sign. I'm way too pretty for jail."

I'd been nervous about this one. I'd never broken the law. I didn't even jaywalk or litter. That was really depressing in itself.

"What if I get caught? They won't let me into college if I have a criminal record," I stage whispered, and he thrust the spanner into my hands.

"You better hurry up, then."

I took the spanner and climbed onto the back of the truck. I tried to remember how a spanner worked from shop class, but when I put it on the bolt and tried to turn, it didn't budge.

"It's stuck. Oh well, we should just go home."

Dallas gave an exaggerated sigh. He took the spanner and nudged me out of the way with his hip. Biceps flexing - I couldn't help but stare- he loosened the two bolts.

"The rest is up to you, Don Corleone. I'm already an accessory."

I quickly finished loosening the nuts and was pulling it loose from the pole when a porch light came on.

"Shit, hurry up!"

I yanked the sign hard, and it came away in my hands. Dallas vaulted over the side, and wrapped his hands around my waist, lifting me off the back and stuffing me in the truck in one, swift movement.

"Get over, get over, get over!" he whisper-yelled as I scrambled over the seats to the passenger side, as a guy yelled something from halfway down the block.

Dallas jumped in the driver's seat, putting his lights on high beam, temporarily blinding the angry neighbor striding down the road towards us. He thrust the truck into gear and peeled out of the street and back towards town.

We were back in the city limits before Dallas slowed the truck. My heart was still pounding.

"How's it feel to be a fugitive from the law?" he asked, grinning. God, he was cute.

"Like I'm alive!" I sucked in a deep breath, enjoying the feel of adrenaline humming through my body.

"How'd you know it was out there anyway? It's not like you could have driven past it."

"I, uh, went home with a girl who lived in the

third house on the left last year." He had the good grace to look uncomfortable.

"What a manwhore you are, Dallas Hellson," I said, forcing a laugh. The thought of him with other women made me feel stupidly jealous, even though the logical part of me knew that a guy who looked the way he did, had probably been sleeping his way through the southern states for years.

The idea was distinctly unappealing, but I was a realist. Not every guy I met was going to be a saint.

"Not really," he argued. "It was just, I don't know... rough this time last year. I needed some stress relief. It was no different to fishing, or that meditation you do. It was nothing."

"Stress relief? I'm sure Tina, or Steffanie with a double-f, or Ashley or whatever her name was would really appreciate being placed into the same category as a big-mouthed bass."

"Well, she certainly had a big-"

I waved a finger at his stupid grinning face. "Don't even."

He just smiled smugly and stared at the road. I looked at the sign in my hands and wished, not for the first time, that Angela was here. She would have thought this was the best adventure ever.

"How about I buy the smooth criminal a sundae?

The diner near the campground does an epic banana split."

I smiled. "Thanks."

A WEEK AFTER LIZ LEFT, Wyatt got a call from his oldest daughter Helen, in New York. Liz had turned up on her doorstep, and she was going to stay with her for the foreseeable future. Helen was going to get the girl some consistent help.

The lines around Ruben's eyes faded almost immediately. He looked ten years younger. Although we weren't friends, he hadn't really spoken to me since she left. I didn't take it personally; I was a catalyst for a disaster that had really nothing to do with me. Despite whether he blamed me or not, I respected the ominous looking man. He wasn't someone I'd want to meet in a dark alley, especially if you were on his bad side. I sometimes wondered if Jonas still had full use of both his kneecaps.

But even though he was built for violence, he had a soft side to him, just as Baba had said. Iris definitely put a dent in his tough guy image, anyway. She was often strapped to his chest as he worked the carnival, putting out fires and chatting to patrons. He was catnip for unhappy housewives. It was like he spoke directly to their ovaries. It made me distinctly uncomfortable when they undressed him with their eyes.

But if the eyes of the mom's followed Ruben, then every woman between twelve and forty turned when Dallas walked by. To watch him work a crowd was nothing short of spectacular. He joked with the kids, winked at their mom's and was just forbidden enough to enchant the teens. The showoff.

News of Liz's safety lifted the residual shroud of unease that had blanketed the carnival for the last week. Everyone had been waiting for the police to knock on the door and say that they'd found Liz's body in a dumpster somewhere.

The state of Georgia was suffering through a heat wave, and today was predicted to be the hottest June day in recorded history. I'd abandoned the jeans and polo uniform for a light cotton sundress. Elise was babysitting Iris, and they'd come to the ducks for a swim. I'd cleaned out the duck tub that morning, glad for a job that meant I'd get soaked, as it had been unbearably hot before the sun had even graced the horizon. My tiny AC unit had not been made to compete with this type of dense, steamy heat.

Iris was dressed in a tiny polka dot one piece, a turquoise ruffle around the waist and a picture of a mermaid on the front. She had a big, floppy sunhat on her head. She let out a little squeak when Elise put her in the water, and I splashed my hand and made funny noises to distract her from crying. Eventually the novelty of the floating yellow ducks were distraction enough and she gurgled happily.

I aimed a puff of air at my hairline. "I wish I could join her."

"I know," Elise huffed, elbows deep in the water. "Once the bumper boats finish for the night, I think we'll have a pool party. Maybe grill some meat and make it a cookout."

The bumper boats were a kid ride where you peddled around a little boat in four feet of water. The idea of immersing myself in water sounded blissful.

A family who had braved the heat shuffled over to the ducks.

"Three ducks for five dollars" I said, smiling politely. The mom lifted her sunglasses to look in her purse, and I winced at her raccoon sunburn.

The boy halfheartedly pulled out three ducks, totally wilted from the heat. I gave him a hand held fan that had an LED smiley face on it. The points didn't quite match, but I felt sorry for the little guy. He turned it on and let out a sigh.

"I suggest a slushy. It's hotter than hades out here today," I told the sunburned parents, who looked about ready to collapse. As they walked on I turned back to Elise.

"Who's first aid today?" I asked Elise. Normally it was Elise running around with her first aid fanny pack, doctoring kids who stuffed their hands down the mouths of clowns, or bandaging up the knees of kids who'd tried to jump the barriers to skip the line, that kind of thing.

"I am," she said, splashing Iris. "But Ruben has taken over for an hour so I could take little miss here for a dip and get out of the heat for a while. I gotta tell ya, the heat really wipes you out at this age."

"Twenty-one?"

Elise laughed and splashed me, which I made no attempt to dodge. I grabbed a bottle of water from the little cooler in the corner, and passed one to Elise.

I really liked Elise, and Wyatt too. He was booming and convivial, and she was quiet, but with a wicked wit. They made a good team, and their love flowed from them and settled over every person they met.

"I keep forgetting to tell you I like your hair, Liv. I wish I was young enough to get away with it."

I thought about Angela and her bucket list. "You should do it. Believe me when I tell your life is too short."

Elise pulled Iris out of the water and cradled her in one arm, and then surprised me by wrapping her other arm around my shoulders, pulling me into a hug.

"I admire what you are doing here. It takes a lot of guts to step out into the unknown. Dallas told us, just the family mind you, about your friend and the list. If there's anything you need help with, all you have to do is ask. We have daughters not that much older than you and your friend. The thought of them in that situation," she shook her head, as if the thought was too dreadful to contemplate. "So, I mean it. If you need anything, even just to talk, my door is always open."

I hadn't known that Dallas had let everyone know about Angela's bucket list, and I wasn't sure if I was angry or relieved.

"Thanks, Elise."

"Anytime, Honey. Now, I better get this little angel back to Uncle Ruby." I couldn't hold back the laugh. Uncle Ruby indeed. Elise chuckled. "Dallas started it and I'm afraid that it's caught on. Poor Ruben."

I waved goodbye and sat back on my stool. The air felt thick enough to swallow. The sun had zapped all the grass and the pathways were quickly becoming dust bowls.

When the sun finally made its excruciatingly slow trek to the horizon, the instant relief of dusk made me giddy. The teens emerged from their air-conditioned houses, frenzied from a day spent cooped up, and poured through the carnival gates. Their enthusiasm was electric, and as exhausted as I was, I couldn't help but get caught up in it. Girls squealed on the Sizzler, young lovers made out awkwardly on the carousel and the smell of corn-dogs flowed on the cool, southerly breeze.

On nights like this, I knew why people become lifetime carnies. It was like nirvana.

Something uncurled in my chest and wrapped around my heart. It took awhile for me to identify the feeling as happiness, and not indigestion. It had been so long since I'd felt genuine happiness, without fear or anxiety pushing at the edges. Without the worries of pleasing my parents, or Angela's illness, and the looming specter of death. Tonight, was I could feel young and happy and free.

The ducks wasn't a popular game with the teens, so I wasn't overly busy. I could watch them show off at the other midway booths, shooting ducks and throwing bushels, trying to win big prizes for their lady loves of the minute.

Although I was a similar age to these people, I

didn't feel a part of them. I'd skipped the giddiness of youth.

Eventually ten p.m. rolled and the teens were herded off the lot. I began packing up my booth, putting everything into the large metal box that would get shifted onto the moving trucks to the next location. I dropped a duck on my foot, kicking it under the skirting of the duck pond.

"Dammit." Lowering myself to my hands and knees, I felt around under the skirt for fugitive duck.

Someone cleared their throat, and I jumped, banging my head on a crossbar. "Fuck!"

I looked up and saw Dallas smiling down at me, his teeth glowing in the white strobe lights.

He held out a hand and I took it, letting him pull me to my feet. I dropped the offending duck into the box, and locked it up.

"Come on," he said, tugging me against the crowd milling towards the exit. The last time he had that look on his face, we'd committed several misdemeanors under Georgia State Law. I knew that for a fact, I googled it as soon as I'd gotten home.

"Seriously, Dallas, I can't thieve any more things."

He laughed. "We aren't stealing anything."

He stopped at the gate to the Hurricane. I took a step back. "I've changed my mind. Let's go and try shoplifting." I turned but he still had hold of my hand.

"This is an end of show tradition."

"Since when?" I accused. I'd done a couple of teardowns now, and no one had ever ridden the Hurricane.

"Since now."

Wyatt was manning the Hurricane, which was usually Dallas or old Ted's job. Dallas took me to one of the seats and strapped me in, despite my weak protests. He sat next to me and strapped himself in. Wyatt came over and double checked our safety harnesses.

"Have a good ride," he chuckled, and walked back to the control box, switching the ride on.

"I've already done this one on the list, Dallas." I slammed my eyes shut, and I felt Dallas reach over and grab my hand.

"That ride was for a dead girl, Livvy. This one's for you."

I wanted to protest, but the ride was beginning to build momentum, spinning as the large arm raised us up further with each drop. I squeezed Dallas's hand harder, but he didn't even wince. The spins got faster, and the pendulum was almost horizontal, and I was only just holding onto my girlish screams.

Then the pendulum arm flew past vertical, and

we were inverted, and I let the scream out. I crushed Dallas's hand till I felt it crack, the other hand having a death grip on my harness.

"Look, Livvy. It doesn't count if you don't look," Dallas yelled and I whipped my eyes toward him. I held his gaze, and something passed between us in the moment.

And then the ride was plummeting us back down to earth, gravity pushing my head back against the headrest.

As it began its easy deceleration, I let go of my death grip on the bars. I opened my eyes and looked out over the lights of the carnival. Dallas had told me that the carnival was lit with over a thousand lights of a night time, and they twinkled like stars below me.

I raised my hands up, Dallas's fingers entwined in mine still, and felt the wind cup our hands.

"Woo!" I laughed into the darkness, and Dallas yelled right along with me. Adrenaline made me giddy. When the ride stopped, and Wyatt released the harnesses, Dallas took me by the hand and pulled me into a quick hug.

"You did it, Livvy. You conquered the Hurricane."

I felt like I'd conquered far more than that.

CHAPTER SIX

NICEVILLE, FLORIDA

I could still hear the thump-thump of my heart over the tinny sound of the plane's engines. I was dressed in a bright orange jumpsuit that made me look a little like an escaped prisoner, except for the harness that was giving me an uncomfortable wedgie. Dallas was sitting next to me, looking completely washed out in fluro-orange. No one looked good in orange, but with his golden tan and light blond hair, it just made him look like a really large cheeto. He tried to say something but I couldn't hear him over the engines and the blood roaring in my ears, so I just shook my head. He smiled and grabbed my hand, lacing his fingers through mine. I looked at our entwined hand and then back at his perfect, white smile. He held my hand a lot now.

Blood rushed into my cheeks, and I smiled shyly back. Dallas had been my friend, my mentor and sometimes my anchor during this whole adventure, but he'd never been anything more than friendly. Maybe that was all this was, just friendly reassurance. How would I know? My experience with boys had been limited to letting James Hugan kiss me sloppily in the back of the rented limo after junior prom. Besides, I wouldn't know true affection if it slapped me in the face.

We'd taken a detour on the way to Niceville, the scenic route Dallas had said. When we'd travelled down a dirt road and I'd seen the small aircraft circling in the sky, I'd known exactly what he'd had in mind. Number 14: Go Skydiving, so you can know what it is like to fly.

I'd refused to get out of the truck.

"What was your grand plan, Liv? To just leave all the hard stuff til last, get really drunk and do it all at once? Come on, you beat the Hurricane, you can do anything."

That had been exactly my plan, but instead of telling him that, I'd begrudgingly gotten out of the truck and walked to my doom.

Now, my instructor came up and made some hand gestures that I assumed meant it was time to connect together and jump. I probably should have paid more attention to the lesson on the ground, but I was too busy envisioning my sudden and gruesome death from a great height. Dallas gave my hand one last squeeze as he pulled me to my feet. The instructor strapped us together and I concentrated on taking deep calming breaths so I didn't pass out.

The doors slid open, and I could see nothing but blue sky. The instructor's hand came into my field a vision as he counted down with his fingers. Three... two... one. And then we were falling. Adrenaline pumped through my body, clouding my mind with a strange form of calm. Right here, right now, I was just me. Not Olivia, the grieving best friend. Not Olivia, who was a disappointment to her parents. Exhilaration and joy swept through my body as I took in the views around me. I could see the beautiful colors of the bayou, the spread of New Orleans in the distance. Time slowed until I was living in just this moment, and I felt happy.

I looked over at Dallas, who was falling parallel to us, and he gave me a thumbs up, his smile wide. I realized I too was grinning and laughing, although the wind was stealing the sound as soon as it left my lips. The instructor did another hand signal to tell me he was going to release the chute, and suddenly I was jerked up and vertical. Our descent slowed, but all too quickly we were at the drop-zone. I prepared myself to land, running to slow myself.

My face hurt from grinning as Dallas landed close behind us, and as soon as we were unclipped, I ran to him and launched myself into his arms. We were both laughing as he spun me around. I wrapped my arms and legs around him and hugged him tight.

Perfect.

IT WAS sad reflection of society that I had gotten used to people treating me as if I was an uneducated loser after the first week. I no longer took it personally, or jumped to my own defense, or the defense of the people I'd come to call my friends. Instead, I just let their insults roll off my back, knowing that these people were just propagating stereotypes to help themselves feel better about their sad little lives.

"Look at the carnie with all her teeth," a college guy said.

"Nah, bro, I prefer the ones without teeth. Better to get a BJ from," Doofus two would quip, leering at me as they'd walk past. I would stare back, my chin held high, and resist the urge to give them the finger.

They were better than the parents who would hold out there dollar bills by two fingers, afraid touching me would give them some kind of disease. I was more likely to catch something communicable from handling the nets that their snot nosed kids had used. I had to sanitize my hands a million times a day.

Fuck them all. I knew better. I knew Manny was sending money back to his wife and kids in Mexico, so they could go to a good school, and maybe get a student visa to go to a US college one day, if they wanted.

At least twenty of the other itinerant summer workers were college students, spread across the different faculties, from Ben majoring in Geophysics, to Jane-Ann who was doing a liberal arts degree. There were the people saving for their dream homes, or holidays to exotic places. The blind prejudice of society wouldn't stop them from chasing their dreams.

In a lull, I pulled out Ange's journal. It was getting fat from photos and notes, as well as other mementos. The ticket stub from the first ride on the Hurricane, a lock of my mermaid hair, a picture of me and Dallas hugging on the platform of the Hurricane, silhouetted by the lights of the ride at night. The corners were beginning to look worn, and the pages were well thumbed.

I hadn't chosen an entry yet. Technically, I'd

crossed off number fourteen when I'd flung myself from a plane several miles in the air. But that feeling of elation was still riding me. I was ready for another one. I fanned the pages, and stopped on one with bold red letters right across the page.

"Take more risks." I flicked back to the picture of Dallas and me, our bodies pressed together in the darkness.

Take more risks. Angela better be right about this one.

I MENTALLY PREPARED myself for my master plan. I decided for it to be a risk, I had to be spontaneous and not plan every second and every word.

I'd worn the blue velvet bodice top, and one of the shorter gypsy skirts I'd bought in the consignment store. It was black and hung low on my hips, just brushing my knees.

I'd brushed out my hair until it fell like a blue waterfall down my back. I'd even put on a swipe a lip gloss before the carnival closed down for the day. I was ready.

"I'd like to play with your ducks," a guy said from my left. A group of four college boys stopped in front of my booth, and I tried my hardest not to roll my eyes. Like I hadn't heard that one before.

"Five bucks for three ducks," I said pleasantly, but I didn't smile. The guy handed over a fiver and I gave him a net. He scooped all the ducks in one go and handed the net back to me. I counted the numbers.

"You've got a choice of a race car or a tiara."

"How about a kiss?" one snickered. They were big and beefy, except one guy in the back with glasses. He shifted from foot to foot looking uncomfortable.

"I don't think so guys. Hellson Brothers amusements is wrapping up for the night. If you could start heading toward the exit, that'd be great." I handed one the car and resisted the urge to tell him to jam it where the sun didn't shine.

"Frigid bitch," Big Beefy guy #2 said, but they walked away.

I marveled again how far I'd come in two short weeks. Old Olivia would have cowered and stuttered. It was amazing how much of a callous you could build in just a few weeks of customer service.

I closed down the booth and headed out towards the dumpster with my bag of trash, mostly failed ticket stubs from the Lucky Ticket booth next door and used napkins. Then, I was going to find Dallas and kiss him.

I should lead up to the kissing probably. Maybe

we could go for a drive somewhere, or I could invite him over to my trailer to watch Star Wars movies on my laptop. Dammit, I was planning again. I should probably just walk up to him and kiss him before I lost my nerve.

I walked between the trucks toward the large dumpster. A hand snaked out of the darkness and grabbed me, another slapping over my mouth.

"I want my prize, bitch," a voice whispered in my ear, "but I don't want a kiss now."

Other hands grabbed me and I tried to scream, but the hand was pressed to my mouth like a seal. I sucked in big breaths through my nose as large hands pawed at my breasts. I recognized the college guys from my booth. Oh, god.

"Nice, just the right size." He squeezed hard and I gagged. "Hey Clark Kent, get over here."

The guy with the glasses walked over, looking pale.

"Clark here is going to take you for a ride. If you scream, I'm going to make you wish you were dead." He flicked open a switchblade and ran it up my stomach.

Hands pulled me to the ground, and my whimpers were muffled and pathetic. Tears ran down my cheeks, and I shook my head from side to side. Glasses placed his hand over my mouth, as he kneeled down near my knees, forcing them apart. He was sweating and pale, and I pleaded with my eyes for him to stop.

His lips were moving as he settled between my thighs, and a discombobulated part of me realized he was mouthing "I'm sorry" over and over again.

"Chess, I'm not sure this is such a good idea. What if someone comes?" Glasses's voice was shaky.

"Do it, or I'll gut you like the fish you are. I'll say we found you trying to rape the carnie girl with a knife. It'll be our word against yours, if you're still breathing that is."

Glasses got paler if that was possible. "I'm sorry," he whispered out loud this time, but not quietly enough. Chess heard.

"Don't be, Clark. Everyone knows these carnie girls start fucking at twelve. Look how she's dressed. She's probably so loose she won't even feel your pin dick. Now fuck her already."

Glasses pressed his body against mine and I gagged as he began gyrating a little. I went dead still. Even though I could see the disgust on his face, I could feel his dick against my thigh.

"Pull her skirt up. I want to see." Chess pressed the knife against Glasses cheek. He fumbled with my skirt, pushing it up my stomach and slid my panties down my thighs, extra hands coming out of the darkness to help hold me down as I struggled uselessly. He unbuttoned his jeans, pushing them down. I closed my eyes tight as his body leaned over mine. I could feel his junk near the apex of my thighs, still flaccid.

He leaned close to my face, his body covering mine completely from the view of the other guys. He put his mouth against my ear. "Make this scream worth it or we'll both be dead," and then he removed his hand.

I screamed so loud, so high, that I sounded like a siren wailing. I screamed and screamed until my lungs hurt from no air.

All three of the other guys looked at me stunned, but then Ruben came around the corner. I saw the shock on his face as he took in the scene before him and then he roared, his face a mash of inhuman fury. He was by me in what seemed like one stride, kicking Glasses in the face so hard that his head snapped back with a thudding crack.

Then he lunged for Chess, who was still standing there dumbly, holding the knife in a limp hand. Ruben grabbed the arm that held the knife, twisting it with such ferocity that the pop of his elbow breaking echoed off the trucks.

Chess fell to his knees, screaming. The other two

guys had taken off into the dark, so Ruben fell on Chess, punching him once, twice in the face.

Manny, Wyatt and then Dallas ran into the darkness, took one look at the scene and rushed in. Dallas pushed the unconscious Glasses off me.

"Are you okay? Olivia? Did they hurt you?" He was pushing down my skirt, covering me, but I was too shocked to be embarrassed.

"You have to stop him. He'll kill him."

"Good." Dallas's eyes flicked to Ruben, and hatred and anger twisted his handsome features. I looked over and realized that Wyatt had an arm around Ruben's shoulders and Manny had his left arm, pulling him off the unconscious Chess.

Ruben was breathing hard, his face red. "Call the cops," he grunted, and Manny pulled out his cell.

I was curled in a small ball. Ruben crawled toward me, staying far enough away not to seem threatening. "Are you okay? Did he…" the words were too horrific to say. He used the gentle voice he normally reserved for Iris.

I shook my head. "No. Glasses didn't want to. He let go of my mouth so I could scream." My body began shaking violently.

"Dallas, take her to Ida's van. Get Baba and Elise too. Keep it quiet."

Dallas looked down at me. "I'm going to pick you up, okay?"

I nodded and he scooped me up like a child, carrying me through the trucks to Aunt Ida's old Streamline. Dallas banged on the door.

Ida took one look at us and hustled us in. "What has happened?"

"I'll tell you in a second. I just need to put Livvy down." He tucked me into Aunt Ida's bed at the end of the trailer, pulling a blanket all the way up to my chin. I closed my eyes and pretended to be asleep.

I heard Baba and Elise hurry in and Baba said something angry in Polish. It didn't sound complimentary. Elise was murmuring softly and Aunt Ida brought me some tea.

She propped me up on a pillow and held the teacup to my lips. "Have a sip, darling girl."

It was hot and burned my lips, but I needed it to burn.

Soon enough the police and the paramedics arrive, and I went to sit at the little table. The female paramedic was nice. She didn't touch me without asking first, her questions were clear but compassionate. My answers were equally as monotonous. No, there wasn't any penetration. No, my head didn't hurt, nothing hurt.

I had bruises on my face, arms and breasts. The

police showed up and had a short conversation with the paramedic before coming over to me.

"Miss Jefferson. I'm Officer Roderick. Do you feel up to coming down to the station to give a statement?"

I wanted to say no. I just wanted to forget tonight ever happened. Aunt Ida was protesting that it could wait until morning, but I was already nodding my agreement in a dumb haze. The sooner this whole thing was over the better.

"I'll drive her down," Dallas said from the table in the back. There were too many people in the trailer and it was beginning to make me anxious.

"And who are you?" Officer Roderick asked.

"Dallas Hellson, Olivia's... friend." He'd hesitated though. Technically, he was also my boss.

Officer Roderick gave him a considering look. "Okay Mr. Hellson. I'll meet you both down at the station. I'll just wait outside."

Ida helped me into one of her sweaters. It was a little large, but it was fluffy and soft, and smelled of lavender. I shrank down into it like a turtle as I stepped outside the trailer. Wyatt had dispersed the crowd, but I could still feel their eyes.

I saw Ruben sitting in the backseat of the police car.

"Why is Ruben in there?" I asked the officer.

"He's just going to come down to the station with us until we figure this whole thing out."

"What's there to figure out? He saved me from being raped!" I hissed.

"He also put two men in the hospital with serious injuries, Miss Jefferson."

Suddenly, like someone had flicked a switch, I was overcome with churning rage. "I want to go in the car with him." I sounded petulant but it was wrong. Ruben had saved me, yet he was the one in cuffs in the back of a police car.

"I don't think-"

I cut him off. "I want to go in the car with Ruben!" I was yelling now, and hysteria was bubbling up to the surface.

"Okay, okay Miss Jefferson."

I walked toward the car. "I'll follow behind," Dallas mumbled. I stared at him with a detachment I didn't feel.

"You should find Ruben a lawyer," I said as I slid through the open door of the police car.

Ruben's head snapped around. "What-" he began, but when I saw him in the cuffs, I burst into tears.

He looked at me, stricken. "Come here." I slid closer to him and he put his head on mine, as close to a comforting gesture as he could with the cuffs linked to a ring on the floor.

Why did bad shit always happen to me? Was I not allowed to have a single moment of happiness, of normality?

I sobbed even as Officer Roderick and his partner slid into the police cruiser and out of the carnival lot, lights flashing.

"Stop crying, Liv. It'll be okay now," Ruben murmured, his voice a reassuring rumble.

"They'll put you in jail. It wasn't even your fault," I hiccupped out, making my tears flow faster.

He hushed me. "No they won't, Sugar. It'll be fine. We'll get this all straightened out." His big, looming presence felt like a safety blanket.

When we got to the station, we were led to separate rooms and I felt exposed all over again. Officer Roderick sat me down in a hard metal chair, behind a scarred wooden table.

"The detectives will be in soon, after they finish questioning Mr. Hellson. Do you want a water, maybe a juice?" I shook my head. Even the tea Ida had made me drink sat badly in my stomach.

I waited for an hour, until a detective walked in. He was an averaged sized man, with mousy brown hair and a slightly hooked nose. I'd have called him nondescript. I'd bet he was great at undercover work.

Behind him came a woman. She was short and

plain, with a deep blue pant suit and intelligent eyes. I was surprised when she sat down next to me.

"Olivia, I'm Shelley Lowenstein, your lawyer. You are only here to give a statement and I'm just here to make sure things go smoothly. Don't worry, just answer Detective Felds questions." She gave me a reassuring smile, so I turned to the hook-nosed detective.

"I'm Detective Felds, is it okay if I film this statement?"

I looked at Shelley. "This one is up to you, but I'd recommend it."

I gave a nod, and the Detective flicked on the camera. He stated his name and badge number, my name and case number.

"So Miss Jefferson, may I call you Olivia?" I nodded out of habit. "Can you tell me what happened, Olivia?"

I explained how the boys had come to my booth, and how they'd played one game and asked for a kiss. I told him how I'd said no, and told them that the carnival was closing.

"What time was this?"

I shrugged. "Quarter to ten, I guess."

"And what time does the carnival close down for the night?"

"Ten."

"So you kicked them out early. Why?"

"They made me uncomfortable."

Detective Felds scribbled in his notepad, then indicated that I should continue.

I told the camera about packing up, and taking my trash to the dumpster after closing. About the hand snaking out from between the trucks.

My voice broke.

"Do you want to take a break?" Shelley asked, but I shook my head. I didn't want to have to relive the moment again. I want to file it away in my head in the box that was labelled "bad shit" and forget it ever happened.

So I continued. I told him about the four of them. The big guys holding me while Chess hurt me. I told him about Glasses, and how sick he looked. How Chess made him climb on me.

"And where were the other two assailants?"

"I don't know." They'd just disappeared. Felds motioned for me to continue.

I told him about Chess threatening to kill me, and when he and Glasses argued, Chess had threatened to kill him too. I told them about Glasses pulling up my skirt and pushing down my panties, then Glasses leaning over telling me to scream.

"That's when Mr. Ruben Hellson arrived?" I nodded.

"He kicked Glasses, and knocked him out. I don't remember much after that. I just wanted-" I stopped.

"Wanted what, Olivia?"

"To be gone," I whispered. That was only a partial truth. I remembered what happened, but I didn't want Ruben to get in anymore trouble.

"Is that what you were wearing, Olivia?" He nodded at my skirt and sweater.

"Not the sweater. What's that got to do with it?"

"Just taking down the facts. Standard procedure." But Shelley Lowenstein's mouth got tight. "So what shirt were you wearing?"

"A velvet bodice top."

"Do you think anything you said could be construed to be an invitation?"

"To be raped? I don't think so, Detective," Shelley growled.

"I just told them that the carnival was closing," I protested.

"That could be construed as an invitation in the right tone," Felds suggested.

Shelley Lowenstein's body went rigid. "So could offering fries with their Big Mac, by that logic."

"I'm just trying to ascertain what made two college boys without records turn into alleged rapists, Ms. Lowenstein. How many sexual partners have you had, Olivia?" The detective asked.

"Don't answer that! Detective, you have crossed a line," she warned.

"These are just standard questions, Ms. Lowenstein."

Shelley's mouth snapped shut, but fire burned in her eyes.

"I'm a virgin," I whispered.

"Louder for the recording, Olivia."

"Stop saying my name. I'm a virgin! Is that loud enough for you?" I was getting angry now.

"So you aren't in a relationship with either Ruben or Dallas Hellson?" He sounded smug, and I wanted to punch him in the face.

"No! They are my employers and my friends."

Felds tapped his pencil against the notepad. "You seem awfully close to them."

"They are my friends. Ruben saved me from being raped. He's a fucking hero!" I was well and truly wound up now.

Shelley Lowenstein stood, dragging me up with her.

"This interview is over. I want a copy of that tape. I'll have your badge for this Felds, you misogynistic asshole."

She turned and pushed me out the door in front of her.

Dallas was sitting in the front room on a hard

wooden pew. He jumped to his feet as he saw us, and he took one look at our faces and his worried face hardened.

"What happened?" His voice shook a little.

"Someone is losing their job tonight if I have my way," Shelley Lowenstein grumbled. "They are keeping Ruben overnight in lockup until one of the attackers gets out of surgery to corroborate his story."

"I corroborated his story." My protest echoed around the room and the receptionist stared.

"They consider you unreliable given your relationship to Ruben and his family." I felt the urge to pick up something and hurl it at the wall. Fucking prejudicial assholes. I felt the small urge to call my father, he was one of the leading lawyers in Florida, but I quickly dismissed the idea. He'd make sure Ruben went away for life, just out of spite.

"I'll wait," I said, thumping down onto the cold wooden bench.

"They won't do anything until the morning. Go home, sleep a little," Shelley argued.

"No." My jaw ached from clenching my teeth so hard. "I'm going to stay here so that each one of these officers of the law can see my bruises and know they are keeping the man who saved me from being raped, and possibly murdered, in a cell instead of the scum that felt my pain meant nothing."

I was born into upper-middle class society, and I suddenly understood how privileged I'd been. If I had been the old Olivia, valedictorian and daughter of a prominent lawyer, those boys would probably be in handcuffs. Instead, I was gaining firsthand experience of how vulnerable girls from the wrong side of the social strata must feel every day. The girls from the wrong parts of town, or from dirt poor families. They had the courage to stand up, make the accusation and honestly believe that the law is there to protect them, only to have their complaints belittled and their own reputations ruined. It was just something I read about in the newspaper, or heard about through the school grapevine. And the victim was always the villain in those stories. She shouldn't have drank so much, or worn a dress so short, or flirted so much. A boy was just a boy after all, he would take what was implicitly offered.

I'd always known Angela had gotten into our private school on a scholarship, but the day she'd taken me home to her single story bungalow, with its Ikea furniture and cramped spaces had been like stepping into an alternate universe, where love was more prized than a ten thousand dollar designer couch. I knew in that instant, when we'd stepped through the door and Angela's mother had hugged her like she'd actually *missed* her, in that very moment, I would have given up everything to switch places with Angela.

I'd finally done that, shaken off the trappings of my upper-middle class life, and I was finally happy. But the brightness of happiness is always tempered by the darkness of despair, and for the first time I really felt like I was no longer the daughter of Lake City legal royalty.

To the officers in this station, I was just some carnie girl who'd lured two "good" college boys into sexually assaulting me. But I was still the product of my upbringing, and instead of slinking off into the night like a girl who had been habitually cast aside might have, I was going to sit there and let the injustice of it all burn away the fear, and the pain and the embarrassment.

And so I sat there, long after Shelley Lowenstein had gone, and even Officer Roderick had clocked out, although he wouldn't meet my eyes as he left. I heard the whispers of the day shift officers as they asked what my deal was and the rushed, furtive answers. I held my head high, even as my eyes began to feel like sandpaper.

Finally, at midday the next day, Ruben was released.

He looked surprised to see us. Dallas gave him a genuine hug, pounding him hard on the back.

"Olivia refused to leave without you."

Ruben cocked his head to the side, giving me one of his trademark weighing looks. He nodded at me once, and I slowly nodded back. He knew that my world was no longer rose-tinted, that I'd had my first taste of the rotten side of humanity and would never be the same.

He collected his stuff and we hustled out the door towards Dallas's truck. They squished me between them and peeled out of the lot.

"One of the boys woke up, validated Liv's story. Said it was part of a hazing ritual for some secret underground fraternity."

My stomach revolted. Bile crept up my throat but I choked it down. I wanted to be out of here.

When we got to the field where the carnival was parked, we found an angry mob outside the gates.

I'd find out later that Glasses, whose real name was Ivan Malkovich, was a hometown boy. People had been proud of the kid for getting good enough grades to leave their little podunk and go to an Ivy League. So when they heard he'd been beaten by a carnie, and subsequently hospitalized, they were livid. If only they'd known the entire story then.

We drove past and we went around the back of the ground, slinking in like thieves in the night.

Suddenly, I'd reached my limit.

"STOP!"

Dallas slammed on the brakes.

"Let me out, I need to get out." I crawled over Ruben out the door. We were beside the truck that held the prizes, big clear bags filled with giant stuffed toys. I opened it up, climbed in, closing the roller door on the guys' confused faces. Then I screamed into the darkness. I screamed and raged, punching the large plastic bags with their hard googley eyes. I screamed until I sobbed with futile rage.

Then, the roller door was up, and Dallas was there. I turned toward the harsh afternoon light and punched him in the face. And he let me. I knew he let me, because he was quick and could have dodged my swing easily, even if it was out of the blue. But instead, he stood there and let me crack him in the mouth.

My knuckles slammed against his teeth and his lip split and bled.

"FUCK!" I yelled, but Dallas said nothing, just wiped his mouth with the hem of his shirt.

Looking at the blood on his pristine white tee filled me with shame.

"I'm sorry, I-"

"Don't apologize, Livvy. You needed that. Hell, I needed that. It's okay now."

And strangely enough, I believed him. I climbed down from the truck and noticed Ruben was gone.

Following my gaze, Dallas just shrugged. "He decided to walk."

"I'm sorry," I said again.

"Me too," he said, gently lifting me back into the passenger side of his truck.

Everyone was packing up, even as the cops arrived to disperse the people from the fence. I didn't think you could run people out of town in this day and age, but I was wrong. That was exactly what was happening.

Dallas stopped out the front of my van. There was an oversized hooded sweatshirt behind Dallas's seat, and I pulled it out. I ripped off my shirt, not caring if Dallas saw me in my bra, and slipped the hoodie over my head. I hopped out of the truck's cab and peeled down my skirt and panties, balling the wad of clothes in my hands. Dallas's hoodie hung to my knees. I walked to the closest fire bucket and dropped them in.

Dallas was beside me, holding out a book of matches. Grabbing the can of gas in the tray of his truck, he sprinkled a splash into the fire bucket.

I lit a match and then used it to light the book, tossing the flaming mass into the drum. There was a satisfying whoosh as the clothes went up in flames, smoke curling towards the sun. I watched the fire consume the last evidence of my nightmare, until Dallas touched my elbow and led me away.

"You need sleep."

I nodded. I was bone tired, both in body and in spirit. He walked me back to my van, and I tried to squash the fear that crawled in my gut, the fear of being alone

"Stay?" I asked, my voice small and pitiful.

"I'll be right by the door. You won't be alone."

I climbed into bed and went off into a deep, dreamless sleep.

CHAPTER SEVEN

WILMER, ALABAMA

Due to our quick departure from Niceville, there were a few extra days before we needed to be at our next stop, so Dallas took me the long way to Wilmer.

We went down along the coast, stopping at the beaches and playing in the waves, trying to wash away the badness of the last few weeks.

There'd been a media storm when Chess, better known as Chester Coulter III had awoken from his medically induced coma, only to be charged with assault, attempt to commit rape, false imprisonment, sexual assault and a bunch of other misdemeanors.

Niceville didn't like when a carnie beats a home-town boy, but they liked it even less when he was victimized by some rich kid. The senior Chester Coulton, that would be Chester the II, tried to hush the media furor, but apparently Ivan wouldn't be bought off and he refused to be silenced.

He'd told the whole sordid tale in an interview with the NY Times and to one of the current affair programs. Apparently the Coulters were a big deal in New York, and the day after the article was published, a dozen people came forward, women who'd been raped, men who'd been threatened by Chester Coulton the III until they'd done things they'd despised themselves for later. The skeletons poured out of the woodwork like it was Halloween in July. My name hadn't been mentioned, thanks to Shelley Lowenstein.

Although the cops told me that I could be called to give evidence, given Ivan's willingness to testify, they were happy enough for me to leave the state. I thankfully didn't have to see Detective Felds again.

So I spent a few days trying to forget. We took my trailer, and made a couple of stops on the way to Wilmer. We spent a night out in Pascagoula, watching a late night movie marathon, and I spent the entire second movie asleep on Dallas's shoulder.

Finally, we'd made it to Wilmer, the night before the gates opened on the carnival.

I headed for the food tent, Dallas going to find Ruben and check-in. Everyone would know now, and I was pretty sure that was why Dallas had taken the long way around. It gave me a few days away from the curious and sympathetic looks, or worse, the looks of outright scorn.

I prepared myself for those expressions now as I stepped through the door of the tent, but I stopped in my tracks when everyone turned and smiled. Not sympathetically, but with actual joy.

"Did I win the lottery?" I asked, confused.

The family, including Baba and Old Ted all stood at once. "We've got something for you," Wyatt said, "But you have to close your eyes and hold onto Elise's arm."

I dutifully closed my eyes and put my hand in the crook of Elise's arm, and wondered what the hell was going on.

They led me out of the tent, I felt the heavy tarpaulin brush against my arms, and around a few more corners until I was completely at a loss.

"Okay, a few more steps. Stop. Now open your eyes," Wyatt's deep voice instructed.

I opened one eye, and then the other eye flew open. In front of me sat a shiny, red Mustang.

"Oh my freaking goodness."

Dallas stood by the driver's door, grinning.

"Dallas told us a few weeks ago that buying a mustang was on your friends list, so we've been keeping an eye out," Elise said.

"Then Teddy says he remember an old man who kept Mustangs outside of Mobile," Baba continued, and I struggled to comprehend the age of a man that Ted thought of as old. Ted just grunted and nodded. He didn't do much talking.

"So Ruben, Ted and I went to talk to the guy and found this old gem. She's a '65 model, and a little banged up. She had a carby fire a few years ago, but that's all fixed up. She runs well now and I tinkered with her until she purred like a kitten. We got her for a really good price because she has a little surface rust. Easy enough to fix," Wyatt enthused.

"Who…"

"Ruben paid for it," Ida answered, and my eyes shot to him. He was holding Iris and his lips were curled into a half smile. It may as well have been a grin from that man.

"Don't worry, I'll take the payments out of your wages," he rumbled, but his eyes sparkled with mirth.

My own eyes watered, but I blinked it away. My cheeks hurt from the enormity of my smile. "This is the most amazing thing that anyone has ever done for me," I sniffed out. Dallas came around and stuffed the papers in my hands. My name was on the owner's line.

"She's all yours. Want to take her for a spin?"

I nodded again, running my hands over her hood. "I just… Thank You."

"Get in the car before you start to cry or something," he teased lightly.

I slid into the driver's seat and ran my hand over the leather of the seats. It was original. I turned the key and she purred to life, and I couldn't help the little "eep" of excitement that escaped my lips.

Angela's parents had taught me to drive when I was sixteen, and I'd often driven Angela to her chemo appointments, both her parents having to work to pay the medical bills not covered by insurance. But a 'Stang was a long way from Angela's little '93 Honda.

I purred out of the lot and waved to all the smiling faces.

"A car like this needs a name." I could barely hear Dallas over the rumble of the engine as I opened it up on the empty road. It responded immediately, tearing up the asphalt.

"The Flash," I laughed, and felt exhilaration run through me.

"Fitting," he said as he gripped the door. "But you should slow down before she gets impounded for speeding, Mad Max."

I laughed and eased off the gas, winding down the window so the breeze could whip through my hair. I couldn't believe they would do this for me, people who had been strangers less than a month ago and now felt like family.

I turned The Flash toward home, and let my sadness flow out the window and into the wilds of Alabama.

THE OLD ADAGE about getting back on the horse was one in which the carnival fully believed. I got called into Ruben's office, aka the table in their trailer, where he was filling out paperwork.

"Have a seat, Olivia," he said without looking up. The events of Niceville had created a bond between us. Sure it was a little dark and twisted, but I felt safe with Ruben, safe in a way I'd never felt with any other person, even Dallas. And despite his obvious attractiveness, I didn't feel anything beyond affection and safety for the large man, the way I would a brother. My feelings for Dallas, on the other hand, were very unsiblinglike.

Ruben finally looked up from his paperwork.

"Do you want to go home?" he asked without inflection.

"What?"

"After what happened, I would understand if you wanted to return home. Don't worry about paying off the car, you can keep it. Consider it a severance package."

I gaped and sputtered. "Do you want me to go?"

He shook his head. "No. You're a good kid, Liv. You have a spot here as long as you want it. I just don't want you to feel obligated to stay. I thought, after what happened, you'd want the comforts of home."

I let out a mirthless bark of laughter. "Unlikely. Dallas didn't tell you?" Ruben shook his head. "They disowned me. I'm not allowed back even if I wanted to go. Which I don't. Those people, my parents, they weren't made to give love. It's like something inside them is broken, and they don't have any need for any emotion outside of ambition. They got married and had children for mutual career advancement. People with families get made into partners in my father's firm. They told me that little factoid on my fifth birthday, when I waited all day for a party like the other kids in my class."

Ruben was shaking his head in disgust, and I threw him a rueful grin. You couldn't mourn the loss of something you'd never had.

"The closest thing I have to a family is Angela's parents, and they have their own thing going on right now. No, for better or worse, you guys are stuck with me."

Ruben gave me another small smile. Twice in two days. It was a miracle.

"You are tougher than you look, Olivia Jefferson."

"I didn't use to be."

"I'm not so sure about that." He cleared his throat. "Anyway, like I said, you are welcome at Hellson Brothers for as long as you want. I know I speak for Dallas and me when I say you are welcome to stay with the family for as long as you want, even after the summer is over."

"Thanks." I hesitated, "for everything." He just gave me a solemn nod.

I stood and turned to leave.

"One more thing, Olivia. I'm putting you on the Bumper Boats for the rest of the summer. Dallas will do the late shift with you." So you won't be alone in the dark ever again. He didn't say that last part, but it hung in the air.

"Thanks, Ruby," I said and ducked out the door.

I laughed as I heard him shout, "Don't call me Ruby!"

I WADED AROUND in chest high fly fishing overalls, pushing the odd kid so they'd squeal as they bumped into another boat. The temperature had spiked above the hundreds again and I wondered who got forced out of this primo job to do the ducks.

I looked down at my waterproof stopwatch.

"Rides over! Paddle towards land, Me'hearties."

I pushed the boats next to the dock, holding them close until kids scrambled out, or were hoisted out kicking and screaming.

One little girl refused to get out for her elderly grandmother. "No Memaw! I'm a pirate. I don't wanna get out!" The grandmother cajoled, demanded, bargained, but the little girl stuck to her guns.

"A real pirate will need treasure," I told her solemnly. "Why don't you go and see if you can't find some treasure over there, Captain." She looked suspicious but finally climbed out, before I'd had to pry her out kicking and screaming from the boat.

The next group were lining up and fidgeting. "All aboard," I said, helping the first kid into their boat. Dusk began to drift to the horizon and as soon as dusk had truly set in, Dallas would magically appear. Ruben was covering Dallas's Hurricane shifts, and I felt guilty about causing such a fuss.

The light changed, the air getting cool and fragrant. Almost instantly, Dallas was there. He was wearing a Hellson Brothers tank. His tanned biceps gleamed with a light sheen of sweat. He gave me a heart-stopping smile and began collecting tickets.

Take risks, Angela's list had said. Look where that had gotten me. I'd almost had my virginity stolen from me, for what? So some guy could get into a fraternity? Maybe it was so that same guy could stand up in a court of law and accuse a real predator, potentially taking him off the streets.

Maybe that's what she meant by taking risks. There'll be times it will work, and times it will all go wrong. The real risk was trying anyway.

Time was up and I blew the whistle. Dusk had well and truly set in, and the kids' rides were wrapping up for the night. I climbed out of the pond and walked over to Dallas.

Take risks, I could hear Angela's voice clearly in my head.

I stood up on my tiptoes and kissed him lightly on the lips. He froze, and panic began to claw at my gut. But then he leaned down and kissed me back. It was soft and gentle and oddly right.

Someone cleared their throat behind us, and we sprang apart. The smiling face of a little old lady with her grandson made my cheeks redden, but Dallas was straight into charmer mode, taking the kids tickets as I climbed into the water to grab a boat.

The smile never left my face.

By the time we closed up, my body was exhausted but my mind was racing a million miles an hour. Although we hadn't spoken about the kiss, it hung in the air between us all night, and I'd catch Dallas staring at me like he was thinking about doing it again.

We walked in silence back to my trailer, only waving to the people we knew as we walked by, until we stood outside my door in a weak pool of yellow light. I stood on the first step, so we were eye to eye.

"So about that kiss-" I began, but Dallas was leaning forward and kissing me again. Not the soft, gentle kiss of before, but a hungrier, hotter kiss. I wrapped my arms around his neck, kissing him back in an equally demanding way.

But when he pulled away, and took a large step back, he looked... uncomfortable. My heart sank to my knees. Did he regret the kiss? Was it because I was a bad kisser? If it was so bad, why the hell would he do it twice?

"Goodnight, Olivia."

I must have mumbled something in reply, because he turned and stepped out into the darkness. I went inside, locking my door, and threw myself down on my bed.

Men were so confusing.

. . .

THE NEXT DAY, by some unspoken agreement, we didn't talk about the kiss and fell straight back into our usual friendship. But it wasn't quite back to the way it was before. Awkwardness grated between us for two days, and it chafed at me like sandpaper. I kept hoping things would just fall back into place, but it didn't.

And for the first time, I considered going back home to Lake City. Maybe this whole thing had been too much too soon. Maybe my parents were right. Maybe, just maybe, I wasn't meant to complete Angela's bucket list.

I decided there was only one way to find out.

After the last customer had left, and all the bumper boats had been moored, I stood in front of Dallas so he couldn't escape and was forced to meet my eye.

"Do you want to go for a drive in Flash?"

He hesitated, and that hesitation hurt. "Sure."

I drove us out of town, out to where the open spaces were wide and the houses were few, away from the town lights until we were rural farmland. I found a field with a short dirt road, and no gate blocking the access. I turned off The Flash's lights as we bumped down the potholed road toward the lone tree. I climbed out and walked around to the hood.

"Get out of the car," I tried to imitate Dallas's deep, gravelly baritone.

"But what if you've brought me out here to murder me?" he asked, his voice a stupidly high falsetto, his hands pressed to his cheeks theatrically.

"I do not sound like that," I protested, but I was smiling. A little of our old dynamic was sneaking back in. It was a step up from the polite awkwardness.

I slid up onto the hood, with its slightly peeling paint from the carby fire. But it was still a strong American muscle car, capable of holding us both without denting. I leaned back against the windshield and Dallas shifted up beside me, keeping a good foot of space between us.

We sat in silence for a moment and watched the stars. It was a beautiful clear night, alive with the sounds of darkness.

"Do you want me to go back to Lake City? Ruben said he'd release me from my contract, considering the circumstances."

There was a long, painful silence that threatened to choke me before he spoke.

"No, Livvy. I don't want you to go, unless you want to. In fact, I'd very much like you to stay."

Again with the silence. I resisted the urge to fidget under its weight. I waited for him to say something more, but nothing.

"So, what? You just want to be friends? That's okay, I don't mind, it was a silly thing anyway. I mean you're you and I'm me and I was just doing what the bucket list said anyway so-"

"Liv. Stop."

My mouth snapped shut on my embarrassed babble.

"You are a beautiful, smart, funny woman. So stop thinking you are somehow not worthy of any man with half a brain. You're too good for most of them, me included. It's not you, it's me."

I groaned. "Oh god, I'm getting friend zoned in the most cliché, teen movie way ever."

Dallas let out a short burst of laughter. "Jesus, have you always talked this much." He nudged me with his elbow. "Let me finish."

I mock zipped my lips.

He turned toward me, his face the most serious I had ever seen.

"I'm gay."

I swear, the whole field went dead silent, like someone had just put us in a glass jar. My mouth flopped open.

"I'm joking."

"Goddammit, Dallas! You can be such an asshole sometimes." I punched him hard and he laughed.

"Sorry. I couldn't help it. The moment was there, and I took it." His smile slowly drifted back to a serious line, and I mourned its loss.

"The truth is, I really liked kissing you. I would chew off my left foot to do it again."

"I'm okay with one-footed cannibals. I don't discriminate. I once dated a vegan, so…"

He rolled his eyes at my bad joke.

"You deserve a much better man than me. But even if I could be the good man you need, the fact of it is that you were almost raped a week ago. I know we've danced around it, and tried not saying the R word, but there it is. You need time to process, to decide… I don't know. All I know is that I'd be all kinds of a bastard to pursue something with you now. Plus you are a virgin and I am, as you so eloquently put it, a manwhore. I don't want you to do something you'll regret because you are all messed up about this."

I immediately wanted to protest, to rant and rage, but the look on his face made me consider his words and the intention behind them. Of course I knew what I wanted, didn't I?

"Do I not get a say on whether or not I am ready for this? I'm not suggesting we jump into the sack,

Dallas." Although the thought had crossed my mind. A lot. But I didn't tell him that.

"Of course you do."

"Then maybe I'm ready," I argued, for the sake of it.

"Maybe you are, but I'm not. It's a big thing, Liv, one I'm not going to go into lightly." He grabbed my hands in his own calloused ones. "It needs to be right. With no regrets. I owe you that."

The part that irked me the most was that he was probably right. Me, who had always been the calm voice of reason was being the impulsive one for once.

I sighed. "Okay. How about we take it slow. Like really slow, until we both feel ready?"

"Deal."

"But no more Sarah's or Ashley's or Madison's."

"What about Beth's and Brittany's?" He managed to dodge my punch this time.

"None of those either."

He slid closer to me and wrapped his arm around my shoulders, and I rested my head back against his bicep as we watched the stars, lost in our own thoughts.

"Dallas?"

"Mm?"

"I think I'm ready for kissing now."

"Me too," he murmured as he wrapped his other arm around my waist and pulled me close to his chest.

He kissed me until the stars left the sky and spread themselves across my eyelids.

CHAPTER EIGHT

HATTIESBURG, MISSISSIPPI

"Sweet home Alabama..." I sang loudly from the driver's seat, even managing to sound in key over the rumble of the engine. Kind of.

The 'Welcome to Hattiesburg' sign looked freshly painted. The city limits were mostly industrial zones and car yards, the odd empty lot looking like a missing tooth between the buildings. Dallas had given me instructions on how to get to the fairground, but I was beginning to think that perhaps I'd taken a wrong turn. I looked in my rear view mirror and saw the headlights of his truck still behind me.

I flicked my eyes back to the road, and barely glimpsed the brown and white animal flash in front of my headlights. I slammed my brakes on automatically, belatedly realizing that Dallas might have been too close behind me. My body tensed for an accident as I wrenched the car to the shoulder, but not before there was a sickening thump, and the body of a cat flew up over my left fender.

I pulled on the park brake and jumped out of the car as Dallas pulled his truck and trailer in behind me.

"What happened? Are you okay? I nearly rear-ended you!" He sounded angry.

"I hit a c-cat," I tried to smother the slight hitch in my voice but failed. Now Dallas would know that I was shaken up. I'd made myself a promise not to be an emotional mess in front of him ever again. I was going to keep my shit together. But then I killed a poor, defenseless cat.

He wrapped an arm around my shoulders, following my gaze to the small, prone victim.

"Stay here. I'll check if it's dead."

He looked for oncoming traffic, but as he drew closer to the small body, it suddenly got to its feet and shot under the fence into a junkyard beside us. It was only running on three legs, and the fourth one jut out at an odd angle. Definitely broken, and all my fault.

"Help me get over the fence before it runs too far away. There must be an animal hospital around here somewhere."

"Livvy…" Dallas started, but one look at the stubborn set of my chin had him leaning down to boost me up. "We are going to end up with rabies because you're a softy," he muttered.

Gym hadn't been one of my preferred classes, but a couple of weeks of hard manual labor had already helped my upper body strength and I found myself scaling the fence like a spider monkey. But once I got to the top, I froze. It seemed an extra-long way down. Dallas flipped over, and landed like a superhero.

"Want me to catch you?"

I gritted my teeth. "No!" I lay across the top of the fence for a second, then swung the other leg over, convinced I was going to fall to my death, or at least break my neck. But I hung there from my arms and when I let go, I landed neatly on my feet.

"Way to stick the landing. Now let's go before we get done for trespassing. I hope they don't have a dog," Dallas grumbled.

I pulled out my phone and turned on the flashlight app. A trail of blood led across the hard packed dirt, and my heart sank. With that amount of blood, I doubted I was going to find the cat alive. We followed the trail, under the stripped body of a VW, and around a Toyota with no bonnet. We came to a halt in front of a powder blue Buick. Lying in front of a wheel was my brown and white cat, unmoving, its eyes open and staring dully at nothing. It was barely more than a kitten.

I bit my lip, and Dallas patted my back.

"Ah, Liv. I'm sorry."

I wanted to bury the poor thing, but the ground beneath my feet was as hard as concrete. "Let's go."

I turned and walked away. No footsteps followed me. I turned back to Dallas, who was staring at the Buick, his head cocked slightly to the side.

"What? You looking to buy a rusted out Buick?"

"Shh," he waved. Shit, maybe he heard a dog. Or security. I hustled back over to his side. "Do you hear that?" he asked.

All I heard was silence. He pulled open the back door of the Buick, and the groan it let out had me wincing. If there were dogs or security, or security with dogs, they'd be all over us now.

"Look at this," he whispered, and I edged around the door. There, in the back foot well behind the driver's seat, were three tiny kittens, their eyes closed. They looked like little white rats.

"She was a mama," he whispered, bending down to pick up one of the quietly mewing kittens, bringing it to his chest. It pushed against his shirt, searching desperately for nourishment.

"We can't leave them here to die."

I didn't need to say it, because Dallas was already shedding his hoody and wrapping the kittens in its warmth. Now who was the softy?

We hustled it back to the fence. Placing the sweatshirt on the ground, Dallas hefted me up and over the fence, passing the tiny kittens one by one through the hole at the bottom where the mama cat had ran through. I looked back toward the Buick, still feeling awful that I'd just left its poor, battered body out in the open where the night animals could get it.

Dallas was up and over the fence in a feat that could only be considered gymnastic. We wrapped the kittens back up in his hoodie and I cradled them in my arms while Dallas was on his phone, looking for the closest animal hospital.

"There's a 24 hour vet about two miles away. They'll look after them." He jumped in his truck and I put the hoodie safely on my passenger seat. I pulled out onto the road and followed Dallas's tail lights. The vet would take them in and find them nice homes and a little of my guilt would ease.

THREE HOURS and three hundred dollars later, Dallas and I stared at the three small balls of fluff nestled in the middle of my twin bed.

When we'd gotten to the vet, the older vet had been happy to take the kittens off our hands. When I'd asked him about how he was going to adopt them out, he'd looked at me as if I'd grown horns and was speaking in tongues.

"They are stray kittens, a pest in this area. The shelters are inundated with litters of kittens. It's best for them and the local environment if they are euthanized now."

"You mean you are going to kill them?" I had to resist the urge to snatch the kitten the vet was holding out of his hands.

"I have to euthanize 25 kittens a week because the city doesn't have the facilities to house all the surrendered cats and kittens that we get during this season. We don't have the resources to hand raise these kittens only to euthanize them when they don't get adopted and the shelters are at capacity."

The result was what you'd expect. I was now the proud owner of three, one week old kittens, which needed around the clock care.

As I bottle fed them out of what was essentially dolls bottles, cleaning them up the way the vet nurse showed me, I looked up to see Dallas looking exasperated.

"What? I couldn't just let them be put down and thrown in the trash."

"No."

"It's only until they are old enough to rehome."

"Uh-huh."

"You would have done the same thing!"

This time, he smiled. "Probably."

"Then what's with the look?"

He pulled out Angela's thickening journal, flicking to a page and handing it over.

"Have three kids and live the American Dream." I looked down at the kittens. "I'm not sure this is what she had in mind. And I'm not in enough debt to be living the American Dream yet." I closed the book and put it on the bench beside me.

"But it's close enough, right? If that isn't kismet or the universe or some kind of freakish coincidence, then slap me with a fish and call me 'Sailor'. The one item that you couldn't have possibly done this summer, not without some seriously loose morals and an accelerated gestation period, and it just falls in your lap."

"Call you what?" I couldn't help the laugh. "I guess. Doesn't change the fact that I have three kittens that need constant care and a job that doesn't give me much free time. I'm going to have to talk to Ruben."

Now Dallas was really grinning. "I can't wait to see this."

. . .

THE CHAIR SQUEAKED as I swiveled from side to side, trying to read the expression on Ruben's face. Luckily I didn't have to decipher for too long.

"No."

"But Ruben…"

"No. The carnival has a no pets policy for a good reason, Olivia. Accidents happen, pets get run over, plus it's cruel to keep them so confined when the carnival is open. I'm sorry."

"But it'll only be for…"

He gave me a stern look that silenced my protests. But I wasn't done. I turned to Dallas, and gave him a solemn nod. He reached beneath his hoodie and pulled out the small white and brown kitten that had been nestled on his shoulder. He placed it on the desk in front of Ruben.

I hadn't decided on names yet, but this one was sweet. It had a big brown spot over its left ear and eye, like someone had dropped a blob of mud on its perfectly white coat. Its tiny pathetic mews and closed eyes made it look so helpless and lost, and I could just see Ruben weakening. One finger reached out and brushed over the fluffy fold of a tiny ear. It turned its head to the warmth of his finger, and that was it. Ruben was done. Melted like a popsicle in the sun.

"Fine. But only until you can find homes for them. And they are your responsibility, both of you. No foisting them off onto anyone else. And they can't interfere with your duties."

I grinned. "Of course. Thanks Ruben. You won't even know they are here, I swear."

He scooped the kitten off of his desk, and handed it back to me. But not before I noticed his thumb brush the downy fur behind its ear. Dallas opened his mouth to say something, probably something smartass. I kicked him in the shin. There was no need to poke the bear. Still he grinned, and leaned over to kiss the top of my head.

Ruben's eyebrows drew together. "Are you two an item now?"

Dallas nodded as I said "yes."

Ruben's gaze flickered between our faces until it settled on his brother's. "Are you sure that is wise, considering…?"

He didn't say it, but I knew what he meant. Considering my near-miss and Dallas's reputation as a horn dog.

Dallas gave him an equally serious look in return, and in that moment, I could really see the resemblance between them. They both had the same solemn expression. "I'm sure."

I sighed. "Look, we've thought about this. We are taking it very slow. Trust me to know my mind. I'm not a child."

Ruben gave one stern nod. "Fine. Now get to work."

Dismissed, we hightailed it out of the trailer before he changed his mind.

"Congrats, little one. You are officially adopted," Dallas crooned at the kitten who was pawing at my shirt, searching blindly for something to eat. "Don't worry little guy, we'll get you fed as soon as we are back in Mama's trailer."

The inside of my trailer was heating up from the hot summer sun. He placed the kitten in with its siblings. "There you go Huey, back with Dewey and Louie."

I rolled my eyes, "We aren't naming them Huey, Dewey and Louie. How boring."

"Oh? What do you want to do? Name them after the Jonas Brothers?"

I scowled. "As if. No, I was thinking Catticus Finch, J.K Meowling and the Great Catsby."

He laughed. "Seriously?" I raised my eyes challengingly as I made the tiny bottles. He just shook his head. "They are great names, you big nerd."

He took one of the bottles and placed it at the mouth of the black and white kitten I had mentally dubbed Catticus Finch. I held one in each hand and the kittens went at it like ravenous piranhas. "I thought Ruben was going to forbid us to see each other, Shakespearean style."

Catticus Finch plowed through his bottle quicker than Catsby and J.K, and Dallas cleaned him up.

"Nah, Ruben wouldn't do that. But our parents raised us a certain way, you know. My Dad loved my Mom, and she was his world. There was no one he respected more. And he made sure Ruben and I knew that women weren't just to be provided for and protected. Hell, my Mom was as smart as a whip, she could have provided just as well as Dad. But he taught us that we were no better than anyone else, especially women, and while we might be stronger, even the hardest steel can be tempered with enough warmth. Women were to be respected and cherished to the best of our abilities."

"Your Dad sounds like a wise man."

"Yeah, he was. Sometimes, even though it hurt at the time, I'm glad they went at the same time. They were so in love, and to think of one living without the other, it'd be like being in a coma, you know? Alive, but not really living."

I nodded as I wrapped my arms around his waist

and laid my head on his chest. I grieved for the young man Dallas had been, but it had shaped him into the strong, empathetic man he was today, and for that I couldn't be sorry.

"Anyway, I think Ruben was just making sure I remembered Dad's lessons. That I wasn't taking advantage of you at a time when you are vulnerable. Not just what happened in Niceville, but you are still hurting from losing Angela. If he thought I was doing you wrong, he'd kick my ass from one end of the midway to the other."

It was nice to know that someone cared. Home felt a million miles and a hundred years away, even though it had only been a few months.

"However, he'll kick both our asses if our stations aren't ready when the gates open. We better get out there."

He leaned down and brushed his lips across mine, his teeth nibbling at my lips, his hand cupping my jaw so his thumb could rub my cheek. When he pulled away, I seriously contemplated swooning. He gave me a half smile, one dimple showing. "I could really get used to that."

"Me too," I said dumbly.

"I'll see you later, Livvy." He winked, and left.

Damn that guy could charm a nun out of her habit.

. . .

"You look terrible, *Myszko*. Are you ill?"

I was perfectly healthy, except for an extreme lack of sleep. I hadn't slept solidly through the night in weeks, and the kittens had only exasperated my insomnia. They meowed whenever they were hungry, which apparently was every three hours. And they were loud. A chorus of tiny squawks was enough to rouse me from my sleep every time. Their eyes were open, and they were more active, so if their pitiful mews couldn't do the trick, the scuffling of tiny paws against the cardboard box worked.

If having the kittens had taught me anything, it was that I was not ready to be a parent. Sleepless nights, endless feedings, having to think about the wellbeing of another living being 24/7... nuh uh. Not for me, not for a decade or two anyway.

"I'm fine, Baba. Just tired."

"Well you are about to destroy a pierogi, so concentrate. Now spoon some of the sauerkraut filling into the center. No, not too much otherwise your pierogi will just explode!"

Angela's list had said "learn to cook an exotic cuisine." I knew she meant something like Japanese or Korean, but I think she'd have liked Polish. And Baba was more than happy to teach me what she knew. I'd learned how to make salads with hard to say names, beetroot soup or *Chlodlik* and babka and now I was onto pierogies. I would have enjoyed it more if I wasn't so tired. And making it in bulk for the entire carnivals evening meal.

Five hundred pierogies later, I was bone tired. We had an unusually early close in Hattiesburg due to town ordinances, so I planned to have an early night, regardless of whether or not the sun was still up. I'd eaten fifteen of those pierogies myself, so I skipped sitting at the dinner tent.

The kittens started to cry as soon as I walked through the door, knowing that I was the bringer of food.

I picked up the box and the bottles and walked out of my trailer. I weaved through the vehicles and knocked on Dallas's front door.

He opened the door, his hair wet and a towel around his hips. A grin lit up his face when he saw me.

"Hey Liv! I thought you were on food tent duty tonight?"

My mouth went dry and I just blinked at him for a while. Then I yawned, and the kittens continued to cry and I shook myself out of my hormone-induced trance.

"Your turn." I pushed the box into his arms, and

walked back to my trailer. I was going to have a fifteen minute shower with the temperature set to "Fires of Mordor" and then I was going to sleep until Sunday.

Parenthood was tough.

CHAPTER NINE

PRAIRIEVILLE, LOUISIANA

I spotted him immediately. Not because he stood out much in the well-to-do Prairieville crowd, although he was wearing a three piece suit which is odd carnival wear in ninety degree weather. No, he stood out because I'd known him since I was four.

When he made it to my ticket booth, we both stared uncomfortably for a heartbeat. Frederick H. Boseman was a world class lawyer, Harvard Alum and my father's most trusted advisor. My stomach knotted. His arrival was a bad omen.

"Are they okay?"

Frederick, and it was always Frederick and never anything as vulgar as Fred or heaven forbid, Freddie, looked pained for a moment.

"They are both in perfect health. I am here on their behalf."

I slumped down onto my chair with an odd sense of relief and trepidation. Then I thought better of it. It was best we had the looming conversation in private.

I plucked the radio off my belt. "Ruben, can you please have someone cover for me at the Bumper Boats for twenty minutes? Over."

"Is everything okay? Over," came the crackling response.

"Everything's fine, just have a private matter that I need to attend to real quick. Over." Let him think that meant some kind of mystical women's business.

"Sending Lorna now. Over."

I clipped the radio back to my belt. "I'll meet you at the concession stand in ten, Frederick." He nodded once, and strode off to the other end of the midway. Lorna arrived a minute or two later and I excused myself quickly.

My pulse was pounding, and anxiety shortened my breaths. It wasn't that Frederick frightened me; on the contrary, I'd always liked Frederick. Well, maybe "like" was too strong a word, but I had always respected him. He was a career man like my father, but had never attempted to marry to advance that career. That made him a better person than my parents in my books. He never spoke down to me, listened to my opinions, and when I was little, he always bought me a doll for Christmas.

No, my anxiety was because I knew what was about to happen. Subconsciously, I had been waiting for it since I left.

I spotted him at one of the folding tables underneath a striped umbrella, two bottles of chilled water sitting in front of him.

"Hello, Olivia. You look well."

"Thank you, Frederick. The hard work has done wonders for me, I think."

"You know, I lived on a ranch for one summer during college. I just wanted to see how people lived when they didn't have to go to a million charity dinners and cocktail parties and all the other rigmarole that comes with being born into wealth. It was the hardest, longest but most satisfying summer of my life. Not that I told anyone that. When I returned to college I made jokes about backwards hicks and dumb cowboys, or just pretended I had been travelling Europe for the summer. I'm still a little ashamed of that. The ranch I had stayed at had been run by good, hard working Americans. Far better people than me or my cronies." He stared down at the condensation dripping from his water bottle.

"Why are you here, Frederick?"

Frederick sighed deeply. "Your father got word about the incident in Niceville. You had to know he would. The legal world is small, and for a profession that clings so tightly to their privileges of silence, they certainly know how to gossip. Especially when the case is as high profile as this."

I shrugged. I assumed it would get back to him. Someone was bound to make the connection eventually, be it the police, or other lawyers or hell, even the judges. My father was held in high esteem.

"Someone owed me a favor and I had a look at your statement. I'm sorry you had to endure that."

I stared hard at my bottle and shrugged. "It happened. Can we get to the point of your visit? I'm going to assume it wasn't to convey a warm fatherly hug."

Frederick looked...sad. I'd never seen Frederick look anything but stoic and professional. He pulled a wad of paper from his tan leather briefcase.

"I want you to know that I counselled your parents against this, strongly. But I am their lawyer, and I am contractually obligated to do this."

He cleared his throat uncomfortably.

"Theodore Jefferson and Augusta Jefferson, officially relinquish their parental obligations to Olivia Jefferson. They are prepared to gift you your trust fund and pay for your college education, on the proviso that you never try to contact them or claim kinship for any entitlements."

"Big of them. What? They couldn't be bothered to come to Louisiana and disown me themselves?"

"I'm sorry, Olivia. If it helps, I believe their actions are reprehensible. To disown your only daughter over this, a heinous crime perpetrated *against* their child? It is outrageous."

"You don't have to tell me. I lived with them for eighteen years. I figured this was probably coming sooner or later when I left. You know how they are, they can't abide a scandal. Their reputations are everything."

The sad look in his eyes was chased away by anger and disgust. It was a very strange pantomime of the real Frederick Boseman. When I was little, I always wondered if he had masks with the same professional yet neutral expression in his wardrobe, rows and rows of them lined up between his expensive three piece suits. In the mornings, he'd put on his coat and slip on his mask of cool stoicism.

"Sign the contract, Olivia. They don't deserve you. And you certainly don't need them." I took the gold pen he was offering me, and signed the last page. I didn't even read the ten page document.

"I'm going to tell you something that I have never told anyone. My own parents disowned me when I was just a little older than you. Unfortunately, they died not long afterwards so we never got to reconcile, though I doubt they ever would have forgiven me for my transgressions. You see, I was - I am- gay."

You know in cartoons how the main characters jaw will unhinge and hit the floor, well my own jaw wasn't far off that. I was kind of waiting for a punchline.

"Uh," was my intelligent response. But things made more sense now. His permanent bachelorhood, his loneliness over the holidays. I put my hand on his own liver spotted one. "I'm really sorry. That must have hurt."

"It was the era. My parents were a product of their time, as am I. But your parents, they have no such excuse. I love your father-" I cocked an eyebrow and he shook his head. "No, not like that. He has been my closest friend for more decades than I care to count. But this? How can I respect a man who would turn his back on his own child? I would have loved to have a family, and he is willing to just throw away a beautiful, intelligent daughter? I cannot fathom what would make a man do such a thing. So, despite my legal ties to your father, I want you to know that if you need anything, anything at all, you can call me. Regarding the incident in Niceville, or money. Even if you just need a reference. You can always call me." His cheeks flushed and the deep grooves between his brows drew together.

"I don't know what to say. Thank you seems inadequate."

"I've known you since you were an infant, Olivia. In some ways, you are the closest thing I will ever have to a child. I am... fond of you."

"Thank you, Frederick. I am fond of you, too. I'm sorry if my actions have inadvertently caused a rift between you and my parents. I never wanted that."

He took the signed contract and stuffed it in his briefcase, handing me a large yellow envelope. "You have nothing to be sorry for." He cleared his throat, and the mask of cutthroat lawyer layered itself back onto his face. "In that envelope is a copy of the contract, details to access the trust fund that was gifted to you by your grandparents for use after your 25th birthday, and details for the trust that will cover your college education. I am the trustee for the latter one, so when your fees are due, just send them to my office and I will take care of it. Don't hesitate to use it for textbooks, off campus housing, anything you might need to comfortably get through college and into whatever profession you choose. I will approve anything you deem necessary. I have no qualms spending your parent's money for you."

"I'm doing pre-med. I want to become a pediatric oncologist."

"A noble profession, far nobler than anything your parents would have chosen for you. I was very sorry to hear about your friend, Angela. A lovely girl. She once cornered me at one of your parents Christmas parties and told me all about a breed of flatworm that fenced with their penises during their mating ritual and the loser had to become the mother. I'm pretty sure she just wanted to shock the crusty old lawyer, but she had me laughing into my scotch for twenty minutes. So full of life, that one. I attended her funeral."

I hadn't known that. My own parents hadn't attended. They hadn't cared one way or another about Angela, other than as the catalyst that kept me out of the house and out from under foot.

"She would have liked that she made such a good impression. She always knew how to make people laugh and she had a knack for finding the people who needed it the most."

Frederick made a sympathetic noise and stood. "You were a good friend, too. Your father told me how much time you were spending with her when she was ill, worried it was affecting your grades. It takes a big heart and a lot of courage to watch someone die." He buttoned his Brooks Brothers suit jacket. "I best let you get back to work. Remember what I said, if you need anything at all, you know how to get in touch with me."

He was so earnest, I reached over and hugged him. His body was stiff in my arms, but I didn't let it deter me.

"The same goes for you. I am now technically an orphan, so if you are ever short on dinner companions at Thanksgiving, you know where to find me. Or you will anyway."

He gave me a genuine smile then, the first I had ever seen from him. I knew this to be true, because amongst his expensively whitened teeth was a gold tooth glinting in the sun. I would have remembered that. It made him look roguish, an impression that would stick with me forevermore.

"I would enjoy that. Goodbye, Olivia."

I gave him a wave and he walked back towards the carnival's entrance. My gut ached. I did those stupid deep breathing exercises. Talk of Angela's funeral had stirred up emotions I'd successfully folded into a tiny box and stuffed into the back of my brain. Frederick had been wrong, I wasn't always a good friend.

I'd been jealous of her loving family, of how easily she made friends, how people just seemed to light up when she was around. How good she was at everything she tried; sports, academics, even art. How she'd seemed to get everything she ever wanted. When she'd gotten sick, I'd actually thought; *oh, it all makes sense now. This is why she had everything so easy, it was just the universe equalizing it out.* But I hadn't ever thought she'd die. That thought had seemed so unnatural. Like the sun burning out. And I wasn't there when Angela needed me the most. She died alone in the palliative care unit, without her family beside her, or me.

Two DAYS after asking the doctor to essentially put her down like a wounded dog, Angela was finally free. She breathed out for the last time when no one was in the room. I had just left her, she hadn't woken at all during my visit that day, and I'd had to get to class. Finals were coming up, and the school would only give me so much leeway, because technically Angela wasn't really a family member. I'd raged at them then, and I don't know who was more shocked that mild-mannered Olivia Jefferson had such ferocity, me or my principal. Eventually, they'd given me leave from attending classes but I still had to sit my finals.

I'd decided to attend the physics revision class because that was the one I was struggling with the most, but it meant Angie would be alone for thirty minutes between the time I left for class and the time her Mom got back from her appointment with the insurance company. I told her parents, and they'd willing agreed. Our mutual anguish had only brought us closer.

But Angie, bless her soul, made good use of that small window of solitude. When they called me to tell me she'd died, I smiled through my tears. That was so like Angie; she wouldn't want anyone to have to see her die, to hear her monitor screech that last long, agonizing note, or hear the call of "Code Blue" that we'd heard so many times for others. When her mother had finally arrived, the last flurry of activity was over, her time of death had been noted by the doctor and she was just lying there serenely, as if she were merely asleep. That was Angie, always thinking of others, right up until her final breath.

It rained on the day she was buried, like the collective grief of the town had dragged in the gloomy clouds to shed the tears for us all. It was fitting. The world was a little greyer now she was gone.

DALLAS APPEARED OUT OF NOWHERE, stirring me from my painful memories. He was wearing a worn grey Hellson Brothers tank, a small tear in the bottom. He wasn't working the Hurricane today, instead doing maintenance with his uncle. The rip showed tanned, flat stomach and his hair shone in the harsh after-noon sun.

"Who was the old dude?"

"My parent's lawyer. Apparently I'm an orphan now."

"Your parents are dead? How? Oh Liv, I'm so sorry." He pulled me into his arms.

"Oh, they aren't dead. They divorced me after they found out about my attempted rape by an influ-ential man's only son in Niceville." I handed him the contract. He briefly scanned the paper, his face growing stormier with every sentence.

"Those fucking assholes." He kicked the dirt, and mumbled some more swear words under his breath before he got his temper under control. "Do you want the rest of the afternoon off? I can cover you."

I shook my head. "No. It's okay. But can you do my kitten feeding shift? I'm not going to have time to take a break now."

"No problem. Are you sure you're okay?"

I gave him a small smile as I headed back to my ride. "I'm fine." Life went on no matter what, and while their rejection outraged me, and hurt a little, I wasn't really losing anything that hadn't been lost to me the moment I slid into Dallas's car.

Dallas, however, looked livid. "Want me to go beat up that stuffy lawyer in the car park? I bet he drives a Bentley or something as equally ostentatious." I knew he was kidding, of course.

I studied the tightness of his jaw and the ruddy color along his cheekbones. At least I thought he was kidding.

"A Mercedes, but no. Frederick is here at my parent's request. He's just an innocent bystander. Besides, he may have just unofficially adopted me." He raised an eyebrow. "I'll explain tonight. I better get back before Lorna has a hissy fit." I gave him a quick peck on the cheek and headed back down the midway.

I STARED AT THE CEILING, imagining pictures in peeling paint like some kind of backwards Rorschach inkblots. Crocodile. Poodle. Two people kissing. God knew, I probably needed therapy.

I had the blanket pulled up to my chin despite the steamy weather. I was having a pity party for one. So I was tempted to ignore the banging on the door, but it just kept going.

"Open up, Liv."

"I just want to wallow in my own depression, Dallas. Just for tonight. I think I'm entitled to that!" I didn't even move from my cocoon of misery.

"Come on, I have just the cure for the blues.

Jazz in New Orleans." I'd never been to New Orleans, but I wasn't much of a jazz girl, or a clubber.

"No thanks. I'm fine," I lied.

"We can go and sit out the front of Anne Rice's house and wait for her to emerge like crazed stalkers? Then we can listen to some jazz."

"She doesn't live there anymore."

"Okay, well we'll go and sneak around a bit, appreciate its pop culture iconicness, then go and have some gumbo and beignets."

Damn him, he knew my weaknesses already. Gothic fantasy and comfort food. "Fine, but I don't think iconicness is a word," I grumbled. He gave a whoop of victory and left to change.

I opened my compact wardrobe and looked for something that was fit for both sneaking around and eating heavily powdered food. I pulled out my tea dress and some black ballet flats. I'd been waiting to wear this dress forever, and now seemed like as good a time as any.

I shimmied into clean underwear, and stepped into the dress, pulling it up over the curves of my body. It fit like a glove. I zipped it up as far as I could, and turned to the mirror. I brushed out my blue hair; it was beginning to show signs of regrowth but still looked awesome. I swiped some mascara on my eyelashes and gloss on my lips and I was ready. The screen banged open again.

"Dallas? Can you come in and zip me up?" I yelled through the door. Dallas appeared and just stared.

"Let's forget about New Orleans, I have better plans for tonight," he said, his voice low and his eyes hooded, leaving no doubt that his plan involved me taking the dress off again.

"Nuh uh. You don't promise a girl fried pastry and then take it back." I turned so he could finish pulling up the zip.

His fingers brushed the bare skin of my back, tracing a line up my spine. I shivered and sucked in a breath. He leaned forward, and placed a kiss on the soft skin between my shoulder blades.

"So beautiful," he whispered. He turned me around and kissed me. It was slow and hot, and I felt as if every nerve in my body was on fire.

He drew back for air but his arms still held me close. The soft fabric of his black button down shirt rubbed against my cheek, pulling taut across his chest. His sleeves were rolled up, showing off the tanned muscles of his forearms. He wore his favorite tight black jeans, the ones that hugged his ass and you couldn't help but stare. I let out an irritated tsk. He always looked super-hot with basically no effort, something that both annoyed me and turned me on.

"We should go. It's still an hour to New Orleans," he kissed me again, and moved towards the door.

I nodded, following behind in a lust fueled haze.

We took The Flash so we could ride in style, the windows down to let cool night air blow against my face. The radio played a country and western tune, the male singer crooning about how he met a woman and changed his boozehound ways to become a better person.

I wondered if people really could change that fundamentally for love. Sure, in the short term it was easy to make all the right promises and maybe even keep them. But eventually, with time and security, people would start slipping back into old patterns. Even into old clichés. It reminded me of one of the associates at my father's law firm. I used to call him Steve the Sleaze. Steve had been a bit of a playboy growing up, rich and entitled, which meant he'd been guaranteed a spot at the family firm. But to make it to partner, he had to settle down ASAP. He dutifully married a moderately rich heiress, locked down an airtight prenup that definitely skewed in his favor, and from the outside appeared to become the responsible associate. That was until he was caught banging one of the secretaries in the elevator.

Warning one. Then another secretary in the copier room. Warning two, because young men are allowed their indiscretions. Both secretaries were fired though. The irony. Then Steve seemed to actually settle down for a couple of years. He won some big cases, pulled off some big deals. He knocked up his wife, and everyone patted themselves on the back for molding him into such an upstanding professional.

Well, until he was caught snorting coke off a hooker on the antique Louis IV desk in his corner office.

Then he took a rather long hiatus, code for rehab, before being sent to "investigate the European market" for the remainder of his contract. The moral of this messed up fable was that even though he stood to lose everything, Steve couldn't manage to keep his hands to himself, slowly escalating his behavior to a point that the partners could no longer turn a blind eye.

Would all the changes I'd made in the last few weeks revert back as soon as I was in the familiar setting of academia, and the impetus to be bolder and more confident was gone? Niceville briefly flitted across my thoughts before I firmly shut it down and stuffed it to the back of my mind. No, that night had irrevocably changed me. Cast shadows across my soul. No matter what happened after this summer was over, I would never be the same Livvy that stood in front of the Hurricane that first night. She was gone forever.

We pulled into the heavy city traffic, both silent as we listened to the nav instructions coming from Dallas's phone.

We decided to park a few streets away because we didn't want to look too conspicuous. We strolled through the Garden District arm in arm, enjoying the night sounds of Nola.

"You know you aren't alone, right?" I started a little at the sound of Dallas's voice. "You have the family for as long as you want us. You have me."

I nodded, chewing my lip. I had his family, for now. But once I went off to college, would it be a case of out of sight, out of mind?

Since I'd signed those damn contracts, doubt had begun to work its way into my brain and I couldn't shake it. I gripped the hand in mine harder. I'd lost one family today, but gained another two. That was something. I was worth something, even if my blood relations were happy to throw me away like bad leftovers from the fridge.

We walked past the antebellum mansions, strolling up to the front gate of the house of iconicness. It was a word now.

In the dark, it was a Gothic wet dream. It was large and imposing, the Greek columns standing like sentinels. I remembered Angela and me hanging out in the public library after school sometimes. She read *Huckleberry Finn*, and I read *Interview with a Vampire*, curled up on comfy couch that was probably purchased when JFK was president. I spent so much of my time lost in books, away from the realities of my life. In books, everything was possible and I could be the heroine despite the fact that no one loved me and I was a scared and wimpy nobody.

"Do you want to go in? I'm sure we could look in the backyard if we stick to the shadows. I know you like to walk on the wild side now, Scarface."

"Scarface? Seriously? It's like you never want to get laid." I laced my fingers through his. "I've seen enough. Thanks for bringing me. Just... thanks. Now, let's eat!" We smiled at each other a little goofily, before strolling out of the Garden District like we belonged there.

I woke up the following morning with my hand still in a brown paper bag of pastries and my stomach uncomfortably round. I didn't know what they put in those beignets, but they had been hellishly good.

"You have powdered sugar across your face,"

Dallas said from beside me, still fully clothed. I groaned internally.

Real sexy Olivia.

"Congrats on your first beignet hangover." He poked my little round stomach, and I groaned. I was definitely going to throw up.

CHAPTER TEN

BEAUMONT, TEXAS

"You have to use two hands," Dallas shouted.

"If I use two hands, I'm going to fall off and land on my head," I snapped back.

"Just hold the base firmly with your left hand and then turn gently with your right," he cajoled.

I was going to drop something on his head in a minute.

I let go of the ladder, just balancing on the second rung, ten feet in the air. I gently screwed the light bulb into its socket.

Every week, we went to a new town and set up the string of large yellow lights that ran along the midway and lit it up like some early 20th century fair. Each one was removed and placed in a special box for transport, and when they were restrung at the new location atop of ten foot poles, each bulb had to be individually refitted. The lights worked like strings of vintage Christmas lights. One broken bulb meant the whole line was broken. So each bulb was checked before it was screwed into the base. It was time consuming hard work, but the result was worth the effort.

One thousand lights chasing away the darkness was magical.

"Why can't you just get LEDs like normal people?"

I crept my way back down the ladder, but each step was like throwing myself backwards into space. Finally, two large hands wrapped firmly around my waist and lowered me to the ground. The same two hands spun me around into waiting arms. Dallas kissed my nose, then both my cheeks and finally my lips.

"I think you might have vertigo."

"Gee, what gave it away?"

"You are one brave woman, Livvy." He kissed me again. Someone wolf whistled from the other side of the lot.

"Is this going to be my reward every time I screw in a light bulb?"

He rested his forehead against mine. "Yes."

"Then you better get out of the way. These lights

aren't gonna hang themselves and I have some kisses to collect."

I placed the next bulb in the specially made light bulb pouch around my neck. At some point, one of the previous Hellson's must have gotten sick of dropping twenty dollar bulbs onto the dirt, or crushing them on the ladder, because they'd come up with an ingenious padded pouch that sat just below my breasts and held two bulbs in separate compartments.

Feeling more confident the second time, I scaled up the ladder quickly, fitting the bulbs one at a time. The string of lights ran from pole to pole in a lazy dips, resting over the large hooks on top.

The warm summer breeze smelled of old grease from the diner beside us, which backed onto the highway, and something sweet that I didn't recognize. After a month of travelling to places ending in Ville, it was nice to be in a bigger city, with more than one strip mall and food that came from more than one continent. We'd stopped at a couple of little places on the way here, Merryville and Deweyville, to do church and school fetes, where we only unloaded a barebones carnival and most of the carnival workers twiddled their thumbs or went ahead to begin setup of the larger shows. Dallas and

I had gone ahead, which was why we got the onerous job of putting up the lights.

Two hours later my thighs ached and my hands had blisters. The heat was still oppressive, even though the sun was sinking below the horizon. The pink of the sky was beautiful but my body was aching too much to really appreciate it. My legs felt like jello as I descended the ladder slowly. I looked down at Dallas' smiling face and realized I'd been conned.

"For future reference, no amount of kissing can make me do this job again."

"Are you kidding? I'm going to ask Rube to put you on this job every setup. I get a fine view of your butt from down here."

I huffed, but damned if I wasn't smiling on the inside.

"Hey! Catch me," I said, and let myself fall backwards from the ladder and into Dallas's arms. Despite what Hollywood rom-coms tell you, even catching someone who was falling from a small height results in both parties ending up in the dirt.

"Ah! I think I broke my ass," he moaned.

Stretched along him like that, I had the ability to find out for myself first hand if his butt was indeed broken. "Feels alright to me."

He just looked at me with that expression that

seemed to make my internal temperature rise rapidly.

Aunt Ida walked past and cleared her throat. I sprung up off the ground, and then doubled over as my hamstrings let me know they didn't appreciate being forgotten.

"Ow! I think I am permanently maimed." Ida shook her head and continued walking as Dallas just laughed at me from the dirt.

He rubbed a hand up my calf.

"Poor baby. How 'bout we grab a couple of sandwiches from Baba, and I'll take you on a picnic somewhere special?"

"The home of another former love interest?"

He got to his feet with agile ease, and I hated him a little in that moment. Then he dusted the dirt from his butt, and I forgave him immediately. I'd never realized that I was quite this shallow. I assuaged my ego that he was also kind, generous and funny.

"No, I went there with a couple of guys a few years ago. You'll like it. I'll get the food if you want to freshen up?"

My hair stuck to my forehead, and sweat dripped down my spine. I slipped my hand in his calloused one, and endured the scornful looks of the other girls in the carnival. I'd quickly come to realize that there were varying degrees of disapproval within the carnival about our relationship.

The Aunts were worried I was being reckless, Liz's friends thought I was weaseling my way into her spot in the family, the women in the carnival who weren't Liz's friends were just pissed because one of the Hellson brothers was off the market, and Dallas friends just thought we were a fling. But neither of us cared much about anyone's opinions.

A quick shower and change later, I was leaning against The Flash, waiting for Dallas. He appeared around the back of my trailer.

"We have to take my truck. Your 'Stang won't like the roads we'll be travelling down."

Dusk washed the world grey as we pulled out of the carnival lot and onto the I-10. Exhausted, I closed my eyes and tried not to sleep. And failed.

I awoke to my head banging against the door of the truck. We bounced over another pothole and my head nearly hit the roof. It was pitch black, and I looked through the back window. The lights of Beaumont twinkled in the distance.

"Geez, how long was I asleep for?"

"About thirty minutes. Don't worry, you're cute when you drool."

He slowed and we rolled to a stop on the banks

of a small watering hole, no more than twenty feet across. The sound of the frogs was deafening.

"This is a buddy of mines property. I called and asked if we could come out. I used to stop by every summer and we'd come down here to fish and have a few brews, before he went off to school out east. He ran it past his folks, they are cool with it before you get all hung up on us trespassing."

I poked my tongue out at him. "That was the old Olivia. This Olivia stole a street sign, remember. She's a rebel."

He turned up the music, something country and western again. The headlights shone on the dark waters. I jumped down from his passenger seat and slid onto the hood of the truck. Dallas opened the cooler at my feet and pulled out two beers and a sandwich. He popped one and offered it to me. "There's pop in there if you prefer?"

I took the beer. I wasn't a big drinker, and I wouldn't have more than one, but after the day I had, I needed the beer.

I took a deep swig and instantly felt cooler. "Can you swim in there? I should have brought my bikini."

Dallas ate half a sandwich in a single bite. "Sure you can. Nothing scarier in there than a few leeches."

"Ew."

"There's just you, me and the moon out here, Liv."

I took a bite of my sandwich and gave him the stink eye. "You've been reading Angela's journal again, haven't you?" I was having a sudden premonition that this impromptu picnic hadn't been all that spontaneous.

"Go skinny dipping beneath the light of the full moon. That's a direct quote by the way."

"You're enjoying my bucket list way too much, Dallas Hellson. What if I wanted to go skinny dipping by myself, huh?"

He slid off the hood and started peeling off his clothes. "It's not skinny dipping if you go by yourself; it'd just be a bath in slightly dirty water. Come on, Chicken, I promise I won't look."

I made no such promise as I watched the muscles of his back flex as he removed his shirt, and the paleness of his strong thighs as his pants joined the pile of clothes on the ground. His boxer briefs were last, and they didn't leave much to the imagination, clinging to his ass like they were painted on.

"Last chance," he threw over his shoulder, his thumbs hooked in the elastic of his underwear. Slowly, he drew them down until his naked cheeks were spotlighted by the headlights.

"Woo looks like a full moon tonight," I tried to

joke, but my voice sounded uneven and breathy. Then he turned around and every joke I'd ever known left my brain. One hand hiding his privates, the other flung his boxers onto the bank. He swaggered toward me, every inch of him oozing testosterone. He stopped inches from me and leaned forward until his lips were a fraction from mine.

"Catch me if you can, Olivia," he whispered, and turned, sprinting towards the water.

I wasn't sure what made up my mind, whether it was the V of his hips, or the close proximity of his body, or the way he said my name, but something snapped and pushed me well into the land of feverish abandon. I downed the rest of my beer and peeled off my shirt and my shorts. I could feel Dallas's eyes on me, and I didn't tell him to turn away. In fact, I found that it was the last thing I wanted him to do.

I turned my back to him, and unclipped my bra, letting it fall to the dirt at my feet. I covered my bare breasts with my hands and walked toward the water, a definite swing to my hips. I met Dallas's gaze and held it.

I waited until the water brushed my abdomen then stopped, releasing my breasts and feeling a small sense of glee as his eyes fell to them and his lips parted. I hooked my fingers under the waistband of my panties, and ran them down my legs. They got tangled on my toes and I pitched forward headfirst into the water.

I spluttered as I came up, holding my panties in my hand. Dallas was in front of me, laughing even as he steadied me.

I couldn't help but laugh too.

"I was going for a graceful striptease. I should have known I couldn't nail the graceful part," I grumbled. "But I managed to strip at least." I held my sopping wet panties in my hand and pitched it over my shoulder back towards the bank.

The mirth left Dallas's face, and it was replaced with a hot, wet hunger.

This was it. I was going to lose my V-card. Beneath the raging hormones and the fact my body was on fire despite the chill of the water, I knew I was ready. I knew if I said stop, Dallas would do it without a word of protest. I felt respected, and safe, and cherished. It was the right time.

He reached forward, and took my hands, pulling me deeper into the water until we were both submerged to our necks.

"God, you are just so beautiful," he whispered so softly I wasn't sure I was meant to hear. He dragged me closer to his body, and for the first time, I felt his hot naked flesh pressed against mine. It was exhilarating. My heart began to race, and I kissed him with all the eager need that was coursing through my veins and pooling low in my body.

He kissed me back with equal fervor, and I felt the hardness of his body against me. But his hands, which held tightly to my hips, never wandered anywhere inappropriate, and although the kisses were anything but chaste, I knew he was waiting for me.

"Dallas, I want you to make love to me." My voice cracked, and I winced.

His hand cupped my cheek, and he stared at me, his eyes boring into mine.

"Are you sure?" His own voice was rough.

"Definitely. This is perfect. You are perfect. I want this."

He whooshed out a breath and kissed me again, trailing kisses down my neck and his hands moved down to my butt. He lifted me into his arms and I wrapped my legs around his waist. He leaned me backwards and trailed kisses down over my collarbones. He moved over the curve of my breast, and then he stopped.

"Wait," he said hoarsely.

"I'm ready Dallas, I promise." I was beyond ready now.

"Shh."

Excuse me?

"What?"

"Livvy, get in the truck. Now."

I stood, confused. Had I done something wrong? Then I looked out to where he was staring. Two eyes glinted above the surface of the water, illuminated by the headlights.

Gator.

"Fuck! Fuck!" I whispered.

Dallas was moving us slowly out of the water, trying hard not to splash around. I resisted the urge to turn tail and get the hell out of the water ASAP, but a gator in the water could outpace me easily. Once we were in calf deep water though, all bets were off. The gator had realized we were encroaching on his territory and began powering through the water towards us.

"Get in the back of the truck!" Dallas yelled, and we sprinted towards the truck. He tossed me easily into the back, vaulting in after me.

I sat up, uncaring of my nakedness. The gator moved around the truck, eyeing us, before slipping soundlessly back into the water.

"That's a big ass leech, Dallas!" I'd scraped my knee on the bed of the truck, and I brushed the dirt out of the wound.

"It must have moved in during mating season.

Goddamn that bastard must have been eight feet." He looked pale. We peeked over the cab of the truck, and saw the two eyes glinting in the dark near the bank.

"We should get out of here."

I couldn't have agreed more. While I was a native of Florida, and gators were a way of life, I really didn't like to be up close and personal with them. "What about our clothes?"

Dallas squared his shoulders, and took a deep breath, jumping from the back of the truck and sprinting toward the piles of clothes and shoes that littered the banks. I'd never seen anyone move that fast. He dumped them back into the tray before the gator had even taken a step out of the water.

"My hero," I said, as I pulled on my daisy dukes and singlet.

"Sorry, I couldn't find your underwear."

I shrugged. "A necessary sacrifice to the gator gods." I leant over and kissed him. "Life with you is never boring."

He brushed a wet strand of blue hair out of my face. "I'm pretty sure it's you. My life used to be boring until I peeled you off the Hurricane." He winked.

We both climbed out of the back of the truck and into the cab in record time. As we bounced back down the road, I looked over at his profile, illuminated only by the dashboard lights and the full moon.

"I'm sorry we didn't get to… you know."

He grabbed my hand and pulled me across the bench seat until I sat snugly at his side. He put his hand on my thigh. "It was the universe telling us that it wasn't the right time." Then he grinned. "But I did get to see you naked, and that was totally worth getting chased by a gator." He lifted my hand and kissed my fingers, entwining them in his own.

Contentment. That was what this feeling was. Like I was where I was supposed to be right at this moment. I wrapped myself up in the warmth that Dallas gave so freely and let myself breathe easily again.

CHAPTER ELEVEN

VICTORIA, TEXAS

A kitten woke me by chewing on my nose. Again. I picked up the little white and black bundle and held it above my face.

"Seriously, if you weren't so darn cute, I'd make slippers out of the lot of you. Especially you Catticus." I scratched a tiny ear, and the thrum of a purr rattled in its little ribcage. JK and Catsby were curled up on opposite sides of my neck, sleeping in the curve of my shoulders. It didn't make for a comfortable night's sleep. The kittens were almost five weeks old, and they were convinced they were tiny lions in the bodies of feral tortoiseshells.

Wyatt had whipped up a small enclosure for them from scrap timber and some mesh. It hung around the outside of one of my windows, held secure by hooks that attached to the top rail of my trailer roof. By removing the insect screen, the cats could climb up the small steps I made them and go out the window and laze in the sun, or use the kitty litter. Or hang from the top like a bat, as I'd seen Catticus doing last week.

They'd come a long way from the mewling little balls of fluff they had been. They were completely on solid food, and it was a relief. No more mid-morning feeds. Or midnight feeds. My sleeping habits had returned to normal. I looked outside the window at the still lightening dawn sky. Well, mostly normal.

Snuggling with the kittens had become a favorite pastime, and within a month and a half, I would have to ship them off to their new homes, never to see them again. The thought made me sad. I'd never had a pet, and neither had Angela's family, so caring for the kittens had been a steep learning curve. I hadn't realized how much you grow to love your pets. When I'd convinced Ruben to let them stay, it hadn't occurred to me that I'd loved them too much to let them go.

I picked up the paperback I was reading, the corner bearing tiny chew marks where a kitten had gnawed on it. The morning silence was blissful. Very few of the carnival crew were awake, except Baba and probably the concession stand workers. Ruben would be out for a run, Dallas would be spread out, baby monitor smooshed against his cheek. Soon Iris would wake up, and gurgle happily until Dallas woke and got her a bottle and put her in one of the ridiculously adorable playsuits she wore. Then they would both come over to my trailer and Iris would grab at the kittens although she was still too slow to catch them. Then we would all go over and have breakfast in the food tent, where Iris would be handed off to one of the many willing arms that wanted to dote on her. Dallas had said that Ruben hadn't heard anything directly from Liz, though their cousin was keeping everyone updated.

The morning routine had become a comfort. No matter what happened during the day, the morning was bound to start the same way every time. Carnival folk were nothing if not creatures of habit.

I couldn't put my book down until I read one, ok maybe four, more chapters, and by then I was running late. By the time I got back from the shower block, Dallas and Iris were already waiting for me.

"Hello Cupcake. Don't you just look like a fat little cherub today?" I cooed. "And you look cute too, Iris," I winked with exaggeration.

"The girl's got jokes," Dallas said to Iris, who gurgled happily. She was getting bigger, more alert with each passing day. And she was getting the

Hellson sparkling baby blues. Already a heartbreaker.

"God, I need coffee." It was a statement and a plea, and I linked my arm through his free one and hustled him towards the food tent. I could smell the bacon from my trailer.

I grabbed Iris's portable high chair and moved into the swelling tent. It was hot, but breakfast was the one meal no one missed. When you worked as hard as we did, if you didn't fuel up at the beginning of the day you felt lightheaded by lunch time. I waved to a few friendly faces, and took a spot next to Old Ted, who was sitting across from Wyatt and Elise.

Elise held out eager hands for the baby, and even Wyatt made a funny face and said good morning in a voice far above his normal masculine register.

"Well, don't you three just make a pretty picture," Baba said as she came up, holding a plate of pastries. She placed it in the middle of our table, and they were all gone within seconds. Cherry danish, my favorite. "Like a little family." My gaze snapped from my pastry to Baba, and my cheeks flushed red.

"Bah, don't marry them off, Mishka. They're young." That was more words than I'd ever heard Ted utter without prompting.

"I was only saying they were a handsome couple,"

she muttered something in Polish, and whatever it was made Ted smile. I'd never seen him smile. His teeth were slightly yellowing from the tobacco he chewed, and he had several gaps, but he'd looked ten years younger right then as he looked at his wife. I could see them at twenty-one, newlyweds who had run away to join the carnival because Ted's family didn't approve of him marrying the daughter of a poor polish immigrant and who barely spoke English. It was an old prejudice that didn't matter anymore, but it had shaped their lives in a way that was irrevocable.

Baba gave him a saucy look and sashayed back to the kitchen.

Dallas gave them both a smile and sat down beside me. I tried to squish down the giddy feeling in my stomach as his hand rested on my knee, giving it a light squeeze as he talked with Ted about some problem with one of the summer staffers. I placed my hand over his and twined our fingers. I could get used to this couple thing.

THE APPEARANCE of Ivan Malkovich startled me so much that I dropped my open money wallet and dollar bills flittered out and got caught on the wind. I took several steps backwards, and teetered on the edge of the dock. My arms flailed as I tried to regain my balance, and Ivan's hands reached out to steady me. I slapped them away, falling forward hard onto my knees, but scrambling to my feet again.

"I'm sorry. I didn't mean to frighten you. I'm sorry."

"What are you doing here?" I hated that my voice cracked with fear. I hated that he was even here, dredging up crap that needed to remain buried. He looked thinner, paler. His jaw sat slightly to the left and his words were a little slurred. Shelley Lowenstein had told us that Ruben's boot had completely shattered Ivan's jaw. I refused to feel bad about that fact.

"What are you doing here?" I repeated when he just stood there mute.

Ivan sighed, bending down to pick up the upended money. He handed the money wallet back to me but still hadn't met my eyes. He stared at a one dollar bill floating down the midway.

"I... I needed to tell you in person that Chester is dead."

"What?" I felt like I'd been gut-punched.

"And I needed to say I'm sorry for everything. I have nightmares of that night, you know? I dream I can't stop, like my body is possessed and I wake up yelling and crying. My parents made me sleep on the couch for the last month because they are convinced that if they leave me alone for a second, I'm going to blow my brains out or something."

"Do you want me to feel sorry for you?" My tone was scathing. Although I knew he was just as much a victim of Chester Coulter as I was, I couldn't find it in myself to pity him. And what did he say about Chester being dead?

"God no. You should hate me, I deserve that and much worse. And the way the town treated you and your friends, I'm just so-"

"Stop. I get it. You're sorry. How did the real scumbag die?" Suddenly, my knees trembled too much to stay standing. I sat on the edge of the dock, and Ivan came and sat beside me, as far away as he could get.

"One of the girls he raped was a freshman, a girl who was there on scholarship. She came out and accused Chester of raping her at a party, and her older brother was some hardcore gangbanger. They beat him to death while he was on bail, and the things they did to him... Let's just say he didn't have to wait to get to hell for his punishment."

"So there'll be no trial?"

Ivan shook his head. "Not unless you want to press charges against the other guys... against me. You should. I'd understand. It's no less than I deserve. I came to the carnival that day knowing what they wanted me to do. I deserve your hatred. I deserve to be in jail. My therapist told me I needed to come down here and apologize to you in person. That I could never forgive myself until I made amends. That neither of us would have closure until I did. I didn't want to haunt your nightmares like that night does mine."

I was struggling to maintain even breaths. I wanted to cry, but not in front of Ivan.

"I'm not going to say I forgive you, because it would be a lie. But I know, logically, that it wasn't entirely your fault. If you really want to help me, you'll leave and never come back. I want to forget that night ever happened, and I suggest you do the same thing. Chester got his karmic returns, and that's as much closure as either of us is going to get."

Ivan was yanked backwards as if by a stage hook, or the hand of God.

Unfortunately for him, it was the hand of a very red faced Ruben instead, along with an equally stormy looking Dallas.

"Get the fuck away from her. Haven't you done enough damage?" Ruben's voice was pitched scarily low. Every vein in his head bulged. Ivan looked resigned. He believed he deserved the asskicking he was about to receive. But it was Dallas who scared me the most. His face was calm, completely neutral, except his eyes, which promised cold retribution. Sweet natured Dallas was just going to let Ruben choke the life out of Ivan.

I pressed myself between Ruben and Ivan, though Ruben looked right over the top of me.

"That's enough, Ruben."

He ignored me. I reached up, grabbed his earlobe and yanked hard. His furious eyes fell to mine.

"I said that's enough. Let Mr. Malkovich go home so we can all forget about each other."

Ruben relaxed his big beefy hand and Ivan fell to the ground. A crowd had gathered expecting a fight, and were disappointed at the turn of events.

Ivan just nodded. "I won't forget what happened," he said, meeting my eyes for the first time. I realized that his eyes were grey behind his glasses, a color I thought only existed in bad romance novels. He looked above my head. "And I'll remember you whenever it rains," he said to Ruben, absently rubbing his broken jaw before looking back at me. "But I'll try my best to live in a way that's worthy of your forgiveness. You're a better person than me."

"As if that were in any doubt, Rapist," Dallas growled.

I reached out to Dallas and anchored his hand in mine.

"Do whatever helps you sleep at night, Ivan. But don't put your death on my conscience too. Suicide is a selfish man's way out. If you need help, get help. That's the only promise I want from you."

Ivan nodded once, and without another word turned and left.

THERE WERE worried eyes watching me for the rest of the day, despite my multiple assurances that I was alright. Knowing karma had visited Chester in the most permanent of ways had given me a sick sense of relief. Even seeing Ivan had given me some kind of closure, so perhaps Ivan's therapist had been right.

Dallas refused to leave my side, the intensity of his mood making me jittery.

"You don't have to be brave in front of me, you know."

I lifted my head from the change I was counting out.

"I'm not."

He stood in front of me, holding my upper arms. I threw a look around but there were no customers in the midway.

"It's okay to rage, to scream and stomp your feet.

You just came face to face with your attacker, you should feel something."

Oh, I was starting to feel something alright, but not towards Ivan.

"Thanks for reminding me. I'd forgotten in the last three seconds," I said, my tone disdainful as I shrugged out of his grasp. "You don't get to tell me how I feel, Dallas. I said I'm fine, and I am. Besides, you feel enough rage for the both of us."

He stared down at my face again, as if mining it for an alternative response to the one that passed my lips.

"Stop doing that. If you are going to hover, do it somewhere else. I just want to get on with my life," I snapped, and felt immediately guilty. He had that same stunned look on his face as the day I hit him.

He turned and walked away, not looking back to meet my apologetic eyes.

I strode to Ruben's trailer, practically throwing the money belt at him so he didn't have a chance to ask more questions, or give me another pitying look. I jumped into Flash and tore out of the lot. I needed to be alone.

I drove too fast through the residential streets, desperate to be anywhere else. I flew through a stop sign, and the red and blue flashing lights proved that stupidity will give you a swift karmic kick in the ass.

I pulled over to the side of the road, parking behind a minivan.

"FUCK!" I screamed, pulling crap from the glove compartment as I looked for my papers. I was clutching it in my white knuckled fist when there was a tap on my window. I wound down the window and looked up into the unimpressed face of a police officer.

"License and registration, please."

I handed them over, teeth gritted. Stupid, stupid little fool.

"Do you know you ran a stop sign back there?"

I nodded once, emotion clogging my throat.

"Do you know that the McKinley kids live on that corner, and regularly play in their front yard?" I shook my head, still unable to look at the officer, my eyes welling.

"You could have killed a child, Miss. If a quirk of fate meant that lil' Stellah McKinley had run out onto the road after a ball, you would have been a murderer. Do you understand what I'm saying?"

Finally, I broke. "Yes. I'm sorry. I won't do it ever again. I wasn't thinking."

I rested my head on the steering wheel and just sobbed. I was already a murderer. I'd killed Chester by coming forward. I may as well have painted a big target on his back. And I felt absolutely no remorse.

Hell, I was happy he was dead, relieved. My hands gripped the wheel and sharp pins of pain shot through my palms. I'd been happy, dammit. Why did Ivan have to come back and ruin it all? Why did Chester have to be a sociopath? I sobbed harder until the cop opened the door and unbelted my seatbelt. He led me to the grass and sat me down, getting me a bottle of water from the trunk of his cruiser.

"Hey now. It's okay. Nothing happened this time. I'm not even going to give you a ticket. Have some water, you'll feel better." His voice was soft, but still authoritative. He sat beside me and patted my back, and my tears subsided a little.

"It's not okay." And then I laid the whole story on Officer Polasky. Angela dying, my parents kicking me out, what happened in Niceville, right down to Ivan turning up and the fight with Dallas. And to Officer Polasky's credit, he was silent through the whole thing, his jaw only tightening when I recited what happened at the police interview in Niceville.

"Well, I gotta say Miss, you are having one hell of a year. My grandmother, rest her soul, used to say that God only gave us the burdens that He was sure we could shoulder."

"My mother is a scientist, Officer. I wasn't raised to believe in God. She believed that religion was the opiate of the uneducated troglodyte. Direct quote."

Officer Polasky scratched his chin. A five o'clock shadow darkened his jaw. He was young, in his late twenties, and I was beginning to feel a little embarrassed at my meltdown. Again.

"No offense to your parents, Miss Olivia, but your mother's opinion isn't one I have a lot of respect for right now. Regardless of your personal beliefs, the truth of the matter is you have lost a lot, but you have gained a lot as well. You lost one family, but gained two. You lost one friend, but gained a dozen more. You lost your faith in humanity, but its beauty surrounds you on a daily basis."

He waved his hand, and I took in the beautiful tree-lined street, the green lawns that seemed to defy the searing heat, the McKinley kids playing in a sprinkler catty-corner from the sidewalk we were sitting on.

"You seem like a good kid, Olivia. You are stronger than you feel right now, and I don't need a biblical deity to tell me that you are going to shake off the badness of this summer, enjoy the good and become the success in life that you were destined to be. You are strong enough to weather this storm, and surprisingly, that carnival out there on the outskirts may just be the ship that will help you through, if you will just let it."

I smiled, and it felt good. "You are surprisingly profound, Officer Polasky."

He laughed. "I took 'Profound Speeches to Reassure Damsels in Distress 101' in my second year at the Academy." He stood up, brushing the grass from his uniform. "Now go on back to your family. And cut that guy of yours some slack. Maybe he wants your rage because his own is tightly leashed."

He walked me to my car, opening my door like a gentleman. "And remember, stop signs aren't merely a suggestion."

"Thank you," I said, and I genuinely meant it. I felt lighter, passing all my burdens off to a stranger who was only too willing to shoulder them.

I drove slowly back toward the carnival, doing below the speed limit. I pulled into the space by my trailer. Dallas was sitting on my step, his head in his hands. His hair stood up at odd angles as if his fingers had spent hours buried in the golden strands.

He looks up as I walk up. "Olivia, I…"

"No wait. I'm sorry. I should never have snapped at you like that. It's just that I'm happy with you, Dallas. I love you, I think. I've never loved someone before, so I'm not sure. I mean, I loved Angela but this is hardly the same thing, and it's too soon, so it can't be love but it's something and…" I jerked to a stop as Dallas pulled me to his chest.

"I love you too, Olivia. God, I almost went out of my mind when you tore out of here, and I didn't know if you were gone for good, or if you'd get in an accident because I couldn't leave well enough alone."

"I did get pulled over by the cops for running a stop sign." A giddiness settled in my stomach at his words, and I snuggled further into his arms.

"I should have known. Once a felon, always a felon," he joked, kissing the top of my head. "But I'm sorry, Livvy. I should have trusted you to know your own mind."

"It's okay. I really did overreact. I just feel like Niceville is this big black cloud that won't go away, no matter how far I run or how happy I am. And I am happy. You make me happy. The carnival makes me happy. There's nowhere else I'd want to be."

He kissed me then, a bone melting kiss that made my chest swell and my blood heat. "Tomorrow is a new day, how about we pretend we never stopped in Niceville? Hell, we'll pretend the place no longer exists, unless you ever need to talk. Then I am here, for whatever you need."

I ran my fingers along the stubble on his cheek, liking the feel of it against my skin.

"No more Niceville."

"Where? Never heard of the place." He smiled as he bent down to kiss me again.

CHAPTER TWELVE

LAREDO, TEXAS

We pulled into Laredo at dusk, the setting sun casting an odd pink filter over the washed out grey of the dirt.

As soon as we rolled into the lot, people unhitched their trailers, jumped back in their cars and turned back onto the road.

"Where's everyone going?" I asked as I watched another set of tail lights leave.

"You'll find out soon enough." He pulled me over to Ruben's truck. Ruben had just finished unhitching the trailer, and was setting down all the stabilizers. Aunt Ida stood in the doorway holding the baby.

"Go on now, you lot. We oldies are going to play bridge in Ruben's van, and I need to start mixing the margaritas as soon as Baba gets back from the liquor store." A grin lit up her face and she cooed at the baby. "We are going to have a great time, aren't we Sweetness? Yes we are!"

"No margaritas for the baby, Aunt Ida!" Dallas called as he climbed into the front of Ruben's truck, stuffing me in the center seat. Aunt Ida just made an unflattering noise and turned into the trailer.

"So where are we going?" I directed the question at Ruben because Dallas was fond of a surprise. Ruben was much too practical for that.

"Nuevo Laredo, just across the border."

Dallas sighed, his surprise ruined. "We go across the border to celebrate the halfway mark. The legal drinking age is 18 in Mexico, so most of the summer crew can party. It's the only time in the whole trip that Ruben loosens up and has a few drinks. Hangs out with the minions. Isn't that right, Brother?"

Ruben just grunted out a response, which could've meant "yes" or "you're an idiot". My money was on the latter.

"Going to a different country. I can check that one off the list when I get home. I'm not sure that this was what Angela had in mind though."

I gazed out the window as we crossed the Rio Grande and officially entered Mexico. It was a quiet night at the border, and we were waved through with only a cursory glance into the tray of the truck and our ID's.

I didn't know what I had expected, but Nuevo Laredo looked a lot like Laredo, but the street signs were in Spanish. I hadn't stepped back into the Wild West, and there weren't corrupt cops or cartel fights on every corner. I hadn't realized how prejudiced I'd been until that moment. We pull up in front of a dive bar, the old neon sign burned out so only the letters P, O and S were still alight. I laughed at the irony. The darkened letters told me the bars real name was Pablos

"It's been that way for years. It's what attracted us to the place in the first place. It's a bar without pretensions." Dallas laughed as he slid out first then lifted me out of the truck. Ruben moved around the front of us, and led the way into the bar, his eyes taking in the crowd and the vibe of the place for the night.

"Guys usually get drunk and front at Ruben, because he's so big. It's why he doesn't go to bars. But he helped the owner here break up a huge brawl a couple of years back, and now she spots the signs of someone getting up the Dutch courage to take him on and throws them out early."

I pushed through the smoke-soaked crowd. "She?"

A feminine voice from across the bar spoke

before anyone could answer my question. "Ruben! Dallas! *Como estas?*"

A beautiful Latina woman leaned across the bar and smacked a red-lipped kiss on Ruben's cheek.

"Maja, I'm fine. How are you?" Ruben's face softened in a way I thought was only reserved for the baby.

I leaned close to Dallas. "Oh. Plot twist."

The woman was kissing Dallas just as enthusiastically on the cheek, and Dallas was actually blushing.

"*Bueno, Bueno*. Come sit down. Who is this?" She waved me down into a bar stool in front of her, her white smile blindingly bright.

"This is Olivia, my girlfriend," Dallas said, wrapping an arm around my waist. I blushed down to my toes, but couldn't help my goofy grin.

"It's nice to meet you," I said, holding my hand out for a shake, but she grabbed it and pulled me close, smacking another red-lipped kiss on my cheek.

"A girlfriend? Finally, one of the Hellson Brothers has fallen. Though she looks far too good for an *el pícaro* like you," she ribbed good naturedly.

Once I got past the force of her personality, I realized that Maja's beauty wasn't the external kind. Her cheeks were rounded like a chipmunks, and she had a small scar across one cheek bone. Her face wasn't perfectly symmetrical and her eyebrows too low and straight. But when she smiled, her eyes sparkled like she knew the secrets of the world and they were really something special.

She grabbed four shot glasses and set them down on the bar in front of us, grabbing down a bottle of tequila from the top shelf. She poured the shots in one smooth motion, not spilling a drop. It was like magic.

She yelled at the other bartender in rapid Spanish and then leaned on the bar in front of us. "I'll take my break now. How is the carnival?"

Ruben muttered "fine," at the same time as Dallas grunted "rough season." I purposefully looked anywhere but across the bar. We all downed our shots.

"Hmm, I sense a story here, but I don't think it is one for a night of celebration. How is Elizabeth? Did that good for nothing *el cabrón* marry her? Did she have the baby?"

"Yeah she did. Iris. The most beautiful baby you could ever see," Ruben said, and Dallas clicked on the screen of his phone, where a picture of Iris smiling was his wallpaper. "Jonas didn't even wait until she was born to run out. Haven't heard from him in six months. Lizzy is in New York with family. Iris is back in Laredo with Ida."

"Ah." Maja sucked on her teeth. She poured another shot into the glasses in front of us. "It is a two shot night. Nothing is so bad after two shots of tequila." She smiled again and saluted us. The quality tequila worked its way through my bloodstream, heating my cheeks and spreading a perpetual grin on my face.

I looked around the bar, its smoky haze softening the features of our fellow bar hoppers. It reminded me of an Instagram filter; it hid all the flaws, making everyone appear more lovely and exotic than any bar in the US. Or maybe that was the tequila. The bar top was well-worn, but not run down. The wood was battered, its dark edges dented and oddly enough, burned. But the top was shiny and clean, years of lacquer and soft cloths had made it smooth beneath my fingers.

The jukebox played a mix of Spanish songs, and the Spanish versions of US chart hits. I had a beer in front of me, something local with a wedge of lime. I wasn't paying much attention to the conversation going on beside me, although Ruben was talking more than I had ever witnessed. I hadn't even realized that he knew how to make polite conversation. He was the quintessential strong, silent type. But with Maja, he was almost... animated. They spoke of people I had never met and events that had happened before I had arrived, so I found my attention drifting.

"Do you want to dance?" Dallas asked.

I nodded. I didn't really dance, but the tequila firing up my blood was making me feel brave. Dallas took my hand and led me to the small designated dance floor in front of the jukebox. On the floor was a Mexican couple; he had a face that looked like it had been cured by a tanner, with a thick black mustache and a small paunch belly. His partner was similarly unattractive; rail thin, with bushy eyebrows that topped a face where all the features were too close together. However, they moved like liquid silk together on the dance floor to a smooth, slow Spanish song. Each step was flirtatious, and sometimes downright seductive. It was mesmerizing, but I felt like a voyeur watching some intimate form of foreplay.

Dallas pulled me into his arms. "I can't dance like that," he murmured, pressing me tight against his body, his left hand on the curve of my lower back and the right one still tangled in one of mine.

"Me either." I rested my head against his chest and felt the thump of his heartbeat against my cheek. He leaned his chin against my hair, and I felt him inhale deeply. I had a small moment of relief that I'd washed it that morning, so it smelled like peaches and not old fries and corn dogs.

We swayed like that for a moment, just doing an easy two step to the music coming from the jukebox. I couldn't understand the words, but I just knew the singer was crooning about love.

I glanced toward the bar, and saw Maja and Ruben talking. Maja was tapping light fingers on the inside of Rubens well-muscled forearm and looking intently at his face as she listened to whatever it was he was saying.

"What's the deal with those two?"

Dallas looked toward the bar and shrugged. "They are old friends, maybe more, I guess. They love each other if you ask me. Maja took over the running of the bar after her father died. The first year was a rough one, the way she tells it. People came out of the woodwork looking for "protection" money, trying to take advantage. That's what was happening when Ruben stepped in. A gang had come in and were trashing the place, starting fights and generally trying to bring the place to its knees because Maja wouldn't pay up. But Ruben cracked their heads together, Maja called a cousin who is a cop, and she didn't have any more trouble. But Ruben, he was smitten. She's a sight to behold when she's angry," Dallas laughed. I could imagine. She seemed to burn with an intensity that I could only dream of possessing.

"Anyway, he came back the next year, and brought me the year after that. They only see each other this one night a year. They have the same obsession with securing their parents legacy. That's why Ruben works so hard on the carnival and Maja is here seven days a week. Neither one is willing to give it up for a tiny thing like love. I know Rube has asked though." Dallas the romantic. He scoffed at the idea. "But I'm pretty sure they bang like bunnies once a year to make up for it, and pine away the other 364 days of the year."

I looked back over, and Ruben was laughing at something Maja said, his big hand covering hers. He looked so happy.

"Wanna go look around? This is your first trip out of the country. Can't let a seedy bar be the only place you see."

I snuggled close against his body. "Sure, but after this song is finished."

He smiled down at me with his shiny baby blues, and held me a little tighter. This was nice. Dallas was perfect. I clinically analyzed the feelings that settled in my chest in a way that would have made my mother proud. Was it just gratitude? Was I trying to fill the hole Angela had left in my life? Was my love even real, or some childish version of the real thing? Was I confusing lust with love?

I snorted internally at that last one. There was definitely lust, no doubt on that front. Sometimes I ached with how much I wanted him. But the guy had inhuman control, and we never slid past second base without Dallas firmly steering us back to safer territory.

But no matter which way I looked at our relationship, with all its improbabilities and all our differences, I knew what I felt was love. *Another one to check off my list, Angie!*

He leaned down, and kissed me sweetly on the lips, our foreheads touching as the final bars of the song twanged to a close.

"I'm gonna hit up the men's room. Can you tell Ruben we are going to look around?"

The stupid smile threatened to make my face crack but I nodded.

I threaded my way back through the thickening crowd to Ruben. Maja was serving someone down the bar, her laughing face softening the harsh atmosphere of the Friday night crowd.

"Hey Ruben," I slid onto the stool beside him, probably with a lot less grace than usual. Old school Sam Cooke came on the jukebox, and the smooth soul sounds washed over the bar. Ruben's eyes only briefly flicked to me, but were quickly back watching Maja's every move.

"You know, I hate to be cliché and all, but life is short. Really short." Now his eyes settled on me a little longer. "We both know how quickly things can be ripped away. Especially anything beautiful and innocent. You should grab it while you can."

Maja walked back down the bar, her radiant smile just for Ruben. "No opportunity lasts forever. Work it out," I said quietly. When Maja stopped in front of us, I gave her my warmest smile. "Me and Dallas are going to check out the city."

Dallas came up behind me and kissed my head loudly.

"You should check out the street party three blocks east. It is why the crowd is so thick here tonight. They are raising money for something or other, but we just love a fiesta here!"

Ruben gave both of us a quick once over. "Sober enough?"

"Sober as a judge." I stifled a laugh. My parents had had many judges over for dinner parties, and I could tell stories about just how sober judges really were.

"Me too. Well, maybe not a Supreme Court judge, but definitely as sober as a Traffic Court judge."

Maja laughed. "Watch your pockets."

With a wave we were out the door, the sun fading over the horizon. The peeling paint of the short squat buildings reminded me of the laughing clowns back at the carnival. Bright and beautiful from afar, but up close, you could see the weathered exteriors and the chipped paint that told of a life lived hard.

We followed the sound of music down the streets, Dallas holding me protectively close to his body in the lengthening shadows of dusk. As the crowd swelled, the smell of street food was thick in the air. The sweet smell of frying churros made my stomach rumble.

A mariachi band was playing off to one side of the closed off street, attracting a crowd of people. We stopped to watch, Dallas's warm arms around me as he cradled me against the front of his body, resting his chin on the top of my head. People danced as the mariachi played, and I watched in awe as the musician's fingers flew across the strings of his guitar with a speed that was a blur. My hips moved of their own volition, unable to remain still against the music permeating the air. Dallas groaned as my body brushed against his, his hand snaking to my hip and his own hips moving with mine. It was electric. And hot! He spun me around twice, my dress flaring out, and then he dipped me, kissing my neck as my hair brushed the ground. I laughed as I watched the crowd upside down.

"Girl, I'm pretty sure I'm going to die of blue balls if you do that again!" He pulled me up and gave me a hungry kiss. It was full of the passion we'd had on slow burn, but I knew it wouldn't be long before we took that next step. But not yet. Tonight was for that innocent love, the kind that wove its way through your heart before your loins.

Retucking me back under his arm, we strolled through the crowd, past food stalls, and stalls selling everything from kitschy tourist crap to fine quality handmade goods. I got to a stall that sold corn on the cob, and I halted. My stomach made me stand in the huge queue.

"I'm just going to look at the leather stall over there. I want a new belt." He handed me a handful of dollars and wandered into the crowd. Someone jostled me from behind, and I shuffled closer to the woman in front of me. She was holding the hand of a little girl in a bright yellow dress. The girl's dark eyes stared at me in that weird unblinking way that children do. Like she was gazing into my soul and found me wanting.

I looked to see if I could still find Dallas's golden hair in the sea of people, but he'd been swallowed by the crowd. It was the first time I'd been truly by myself in a crowd since what happened in Niceville.

Panic crept into my gut as the crowd seemed to get thicker and the shadows darker.

I counted to ten, forwards and backwards. *Just breathe. There is nothing to worry about. They are just people having fun. There is nothing to worry about. I am fine. I am fine.*

I kept chanting the words to myself. Logically I knew I probably should have had a bit of therapy after what happened, but I was desperate to put it in the past. Because that is where it was. In the past. Forever.

The kid's eyes were still staring at me, shining almost black in the fading light. I stared back, anchoring myself to the present with that kid.

And then she smiled. A small gentle smile, like you'd give a scared puppy. It was then I realized my panic must have shown on my face. I continued to stare at the little girl, and she continued to smile. Eventually, I could only see the little girl, with her smudged, sticky cheeks, and her long long eyelashes, and not the ghosts of my past.

When my heartbeat slowed, and the sounds around me reached normal levels, I gave her a smile back.

"*Gracias.*"

She shrugged and smiled, turning away with her mother. I gave her a tiny finger wave, and she waved her corn cob back at me.

I stepped to the front of the line, and held up two fingers. They slathered my corn cob with mayo, lime juice and paprika, wrapping the bundle up in aluminum foil.

Dallas returned just in time to grab his cob and I handed him his change

"Did you find anything you like?" I was happy that my voice didn't reflect my almost-breakdown.

"Nah, they were all a bit to ostentatious for me."

We sat down on a long wooden bench, the bright blue paint so old and chipped that flecks of it stuck to the back of my thighs. I ate my corn, the sweet juices squirting every which way. Eating fresh corn definitely needed a splash zone. And maybe a bib.

We strolled around some more watching the street performers, including one guy who breathed fire, and got caught up in the joy of the festival. People danced, old men complimented me on my beauty, and children ran around with balloons on their wrists and sugared confections in their hands. I bought a day of the dead skull, in Angela's favorite red, with bright white and yellow flowers adorning its shiny surface.

Eventually, as the evening wore on, the vibe of

the crowd shifted. As people poured out of the bars, the children and the elderly were hustled home. The fiesta became a raucous party, and I was ready to leave. I had never been much of a partier, and it wasn't something I wanted to try now, in a different country.

"Can we head back to Maja's bar?"

"I was about to suggest the same thing." He might not be as big as Ruben, but he was still tall, lean and stood out like a sore thumb in the crowd. Already the drunks, desperate for a fight to end the night, were giving him the side eye.

We hurried home, sticking to the well-lit streets. Although I'd had fun, I was glad to be back to the relative safety of Maja's place. The big clock on the wall said it was nearly midnight.

There was an even thicker crowd in the bar now, and there were two new bartenders behind the bar. Dallas went up to a younger guy, who was maybe twenty-one or so, and gave him a wide grin and a handshake.

"Dallas! How's it going, bro?" Unlike Maja, there was no hint of an accent in the guy's voice. He could have been a beach boy from California.

"J-Man! I'm great. Couldn't be better. How's school?"

"Schools great. I graduate next year. A fully

fledged architect. Who's the pretty girl? Obviously not your girlfriend because she is way too hot for you!"

I laughed. "This is my girlfriend, Olivia. Olivia, this is J, Maja's baby cousin."

"It's short for Jesus, but call me J. Everyone does. Otherwise every time I get a fine young lady into bed, and they start screaming, 'Oh, Jesus, yes!' I don't have to stop and tell them that it's pronounced Hey-Zeus. Ruins my flow." He winked, and I blushed a deep shade of red.

Dallas laughed. "That's an awful lot of conversation to have in a minute, man."

J reached over and punched Dallas in the arm. "Careful, or I'll have you black banned. She left me in charge you know!"

I sat down on a stool. "I was going to ask where Ruben is, but I guess that explains that." I blushed again, but the boys just had matching knowing looks.

"Yeah, Maja went home early, despite the crowd. She said to pull Rubens truck around the back and park it in the garage. She said you and Olivia are welcome to sleep in the living room, she'll leave you out some blankets and pillows." He reached under the bar and pulled out Ruben's car keys.

Dallas' face screwed up. "And listen to them bang

all night? Nah, it's okay. We might camp in the truck, so I'll take her up on the blankets. Maja has a little one bedroom apartment at the back of the bar," he explained to me. Yeah, listing to Ruben have sex didn't sound like fun to me either.

"I'll just move the truck now, and then we'll have a couple more drinks. Trust me, sleeping in the truck is much more comfortable if you are sufficiently inebriated. Can you just keep an eye on Olivia for me?" I raised my eyebrows. What the hell was I? A puppy?

J nodded, and Dallas strode out.

"Ah, that's the gringo's first mistake, trusting me with his beautiful girlfriend. You know what they say about us Latinos, we have the rhythm of love in our blood."

I laughed. He was a terrible flirt, and not very good with pick up lines. "Is that what they say?"

"Do now. How long have you and Dallas been dating?"

I shook my head. "Not long, but it feels like forever."

"Because he's such a boring bastard?"

I laughed, and watched him mix a cocktail. He poured it into a margarita glass. "I call this one 'South of the Border'. It's basically tequila, vodka and white rum with orange and pineapple juice, and a touch of grenadine."

I took a small sip, and was pleasantly surprised when it went down smooth. He poured another one for Dallas, and put half a dozen cherries and several pink umbrellas in it. "Dude's so macho, the women just pant all over him. Need to even out the playing field." He gave me another wink and went down to grab a couple of beers for a guy waving a fifty around like it was Excalibur.

A body slid onto the stool beside me, and I turned to smile at Dallas. My smile froze on my face when I realized it wasn't him at all, but a stranger. He was handsome in a too suave kind of way.

"What is a beautiful *señorita* like you doing sitting alone?"

I shifted a little further away on my stool, angling my legs toward the bar. "I'm not alone, just waiting for my boyfriend."

The man scooted a little closer, closing the gap between us. "Well, he is a stupid man for leaving such a delicate flower alone in a bar such as this." He was too close and I couldn't shift further away without sitting on the lap of the guy beside me.

I turned and saw J moving down the bar towards me. "Get out of her face, man, the lady isn't interested. Keep up that behavior and I'll boot your ass."

He signaled to a bouncer on the door, tapping his eye and pointing to the Don Juan who was vacating my personal space.

He walked away, mumbling something that didn't sound very friendly in Spanish. "Sorry, Olivia. You 'kay?"

I gave him a tight, fake smile. "Yeah, I'm all good." Dallas walked through the back door and I gave him a sunnier smile.

"All parked. All I can hear from Maja's house is the Mexican equivalent of Barry Mannilow. I hustled back here as fast as I could." Not fast enough, but I wouldn't tell him that. No one needed the bloodshed tonight.

Dallas looked down at his frou-frou drink. "This looks like a Care Bear threw up in a margarita glass." He downed the drink in one go. "Tastes good though. My compliments to the chef."

He gave J a fist bump, and the bartender handed him a beer. Dallas handed J a fifty.

"Nah, it's on the house."

"Consider it a tip then." He reached over and stuffed it in J's top pocket. "Buy some of those fancy pencils that architects use."

"They are just average pencils, man. Besides, it all done on computer these days anyway." But he left the fifty where it was. J gave us a wave as he went back to tending bar.

"So, how are you liking your first trip out of the country?" He put a hand on my knee, and I put my hand on his, rubbing a thumb across his knuckles.

"It's been wonderful. Thank you for bringing me."

"Anything for you. Besides, normally Ruben just leaves me here to fend for myself. I spend the night sitting by myself in the corner."

My eyebrows rose. "By yourself, huh?"

"Well, at least for a little while." He lifted his hand and kissed my knuckles. "This is better though."

"You say all the right things, Dallas Hellson. How could any girl resist you?" I laughed, leaning in to kiss him.

"I'm glad you didn't, Olivia Jefferson. Now tell me about all the great things you are going to do with your life."

It had been something I'd been thinking about. Although I always intended to go to medical school, I hadn't decided on which specialty I had wanted to pursue until pediatric oncology had just popped out of my mouth talking to Frederick. But the decision felt right somehow. When I laid awake at night in my trailer, with the night noises of the carnival around me, I wondered who Olivia Jefferson would have been if Angela hadn't died. Would I be going to Harvard instead of Stanford? Would I be doing law because that would make my parents happy? What if my parents had been open and loving people, and Angela and I had just been acquaintances instead of almost sisters? Who would I be then? I'd trip my way down the rabbit hole of 'what-ifs' until my brain exhausted itself and I could finally sleep.

I explained all about Stanford to Dallas, even though it meant that my time with Hellson Brothers, and especially with him, was coming to a close. I didn't want to think what that would mean. I wasn't ready to give up my idyllic romance just yet.

"It shounds...sounds pertfects," he slurred. I shot up in my chair. Dallas' gaze was unfocused, and he was swaying a little on his stool. He was still nursing the one beer, and I had drunk the same cocktail and while I was tipsy, I was nowhere near that drunk.

Something was wrong.

"J!" I shouted over the crowd. J jogged down the bar towards us.

"Something's wrong with Dallas." The man in question smiled goofily at us, but had a hard time holding his head up.

"Son of a bitch. He's been roofied."

"What? I didn't roofie him!"

J laughed. "Girl, I don't think you'd need to drug

Dallas to get into his pants. No, my bet is that that sleazy fuck who was trying to pick you up thought Dallas' cocktail was yours. Slimy motherfucker."

J waved over the bouncer, and when the giant of a man came over, yelled something in his ear. Dallas was starting to lean further to the left; a few inches more and he was going to end up on the floor.

The bouncer strode away, and moments later I saw he had the lothario from earlier in a chicken wing hold, his wrist halfway up the middle of his back. The girl he had been sitting with was swaying haphazardly on her own barstool.

"He drugged that girl, too. You need to help her."

J swore again.

"I'll find her friends then I'll help you get Dallas back to your truck." He ducked around the bar, heading over to the girl. I watched as he searched the crowd for her friends, before a sober looking woman came over, and stared at her friend with concern. She went and grabbed two more woman and a man, and they picked up the drugged woman between them and led her out of the bar. The big bouncer escorted them.

With a quick word to the other bartender, J was back with us, putting his shoulder under Dallas's arm and hoisting him to his feet.

I was infuriated. I wanted to track down that

asshole and go at him with Maja's baseball bat.

I hadn't realized I was venting out loud until J laughed. "The guy was lucky that Maja wasn't working, or you might have had to get in line. Come on, Big Guy, let's get you back to your truck. *Dios*, you weigh a ton. You need to lay off the corn dogs."

Dallas slurred a retort as I held open the door to the back. We walked through a kitchen and out a heavy metal door, with two deadbolts. Beside the door was a set of stairs that ran upstairs, probably to Maja's apartment.

I opened up the big doors to the garage and then the passenger door. Between the two of us, we got Dallas's uncooperative body into the passenger seat.

J disappeared and reappeared with a multicolor quilt and two handwoven blankets, as well as two overstuffed pillows.

Dallas was lying on his back mumbling incoherently.

"Should I get Ruben?" I didn't know jack about what to do with someone who's been drugged.

"Nah. We see it a lot. He'll sleep it off, just make sure he doesn't have an allergic reaction to it, or doesn't puke while he's on his back. He should be good by tomorrow. Don't let him drive home."

"Thanks J."

"It's all good. You're good for him. He looks at

you like you're a treasure. Plus, with him off the market, there might be some love for the rest of us."

"That's me; Olivia Jefferson, love philanthropist."

J squeezed my arm and we said our quick good-byes as he raced back to the bar.

I hopped into the driver's side, spreading a blanket over my legs. I lifted Dallas's head into my lap and reclined the seat back as far as it would go, tucking a pillow behind my head. Not exactly comfortable for either us considering he was too long for the bench seat and I was scrunched up under the steering wheel but we would make do.

"I can't move." He sounded a little panicked. I brushed the soft waves of his blonde hair off of his forehead.

"You'll be okay tomorrow. I promise you. Just sleep."

He nodded, closing his eyes and letting out a deep sigh. My left thigh was going numb, but I got as comfortable as possible, double checked the doors were locked, and drifted off to sleep.

THE SOUND of someone knocking on the window woke me.

Ruben smiled down at me. At first I thought I was still dreaming because I'd never seen Ruben smile like that. But then I realized I needed to pee, so it probably wasn't a dream.

"Big night? Wake Sleeping Beauty so we can get on the road. You have the keys."

I nudged Dallas, who opened one eye, then the other. Unlocking the door, I opened it and slid out.

"He was roofied." Rubens eyebrows lowered and his smile disappeared. I felt kinda sad as it vanished.

I climbed into the passenger seat, pushing Dallas over.

"What the hell happened last night?" Dallas's voice was raw.

"Someone tried to drug me, but got your drink instead and I spent all night defending your virtue in the front seat of a truck."

"There really is a first time for everything," Ruben laughed. Actually laughed. He placed the folded linen on a long bench that ran one side of the garage, whistling like one of the seven dwarfs.

"You're kind of scary when you're all sexed up," I grumbled.

"You're kind of grumpy when you tired and hungover," he retorted. He slid into the driver's seat, cranked the radio volume up and sang along to an AC/DC song.

I glared daggers at them both, and tried to go back to sleep.

CHAPTER THIRTEEN

ODESSA, TEXAS

I t rained the first day in Odessa. Not just a light shower, but torrential rains of biblical proportions. In August. In West Texas! I couldn't work out who was more surprised, the weatherman or me.

The sports field where we were supposed to set up quickly turned into a quagmire, and I sank an inch into the ground with every step. None of the rides could go up for another two days, when the rain was forecast to clear. It didn't stop Ruben from staring at the weather app on his phone and praying for a rainbow. Everyone was pretty much house-bound, and for the tent city, as the family liked to call the area where the seasonal workers slept in a large campground, the constant damp and inability to even move around was seriously heating up some tempers.

Most drifted off to spend as much time as they could in malls and bars, keeping dry. The others found refuge in Baba's mess tent. Baba took advantage of so many extra hands, and that night we had a feast. Dumplings, stews, different kinds of breads and pastries and so very many cakes adorned the large trestle tables. Wyatt played a movie on the interior wall of the tent, although it was sometimes hard to hear over the pounding rain.

By the second day, even I was going nuts.

"How about we clear some things off your bucket list. How many are left?" Dallas said listlessly, using his hands to wrestle with the kittens.

I got out Angela's journal from the drawer. I didn't carry it with me everywhere now. It had too many memories wrapped in it to accidentally lose it.

"Five. But there's a reason that I left them until last. They are impossible. Except maybe this one."

I pointed to a page where Angela had drawn an old school pin-up girl dressed like a sailor.

"Oh yeah. I know just the guy. But you might want to wear something loose."

I threw on a peasant skirt and a loose, off the shoulder blouse in a white cheesecloth. Despite the rain, the weather was still really steamy. We raced to the car, getting drenched in that five seconds between the front door and the passenger seat. Dallas drove us through the wet streets of Odessa, and I watched helplessly as the water that had gathered on the sides of the road splashed up onto pedestrians picking their way down the sidewalk. Eventually we pulled up in front of a modest brick building. The sign swinging backwards and forwards in the heavy weather read "Tattoos by Tommy". Dallas found a park and we raced to the large black awning.

"Tommy spent a couple of years on the road with us to save up for this place. He and my dad were childhood friends. He'd do the carnival during the day and ink at night. He is really good, and getting ink by Tommy became kind of a status thing in the towns we visited. I was too young to get one and besides, my parents would have flipped it."

The bell over the door tinkled as we entered, the little brass dome seeming innocuous against the heavy black walls painted with graffiti scenes of Saint George and his dragon in a battle. The art was amazing. The perception of who was winning that battle changed depending on where you were in the room. As we walked in, it looked as if the knight was winning, standing tall with his shining sword aloft. But when we got to the counter, I turned to study it properly, and the battle had turned, the dragon looked more fierce, standing on his hind legs, its maw opened to breathe fire on Saint George. I moved to stand in the middle of the room, only to find the battle had just begun.

An older man, with a long grey beard and a hipster haircut came to stand behind the counter. "Can I help... Dallas? Dallas Hellson? Damn you are the spitting image of your daddy at your age." He moved around the counter and wrapped his arms around Dallas. They shared a man hug, lots of back slapping. "I haven't seen you since... uh, how you been?"

"The funeral. Yeah. I've been good. The carnival has been good, too. Ruben takes it very seriously." Dallas' warm grin set Tommy at ease.

"Always such a serious kid, that one. Even as a boy. I knew your dad's legacy was going to be in safe hands with you three. What brings you to my shop?"

Dallas wrapped an arm around my shoulders. "This is my girl. She'd like a tattoo."

Tommy looked down at me from a great height. He must have almost been as tall as Ruben. His blue eyes sparkled with intelligence, and maybe a little bit of the devil in there.

"You aren't going to get this punk's name written

across your ass, are you? Because I'm gonna have to politely refuse that request."

"No freakin' way! I was going to get it on my neck so everyone can see who I belong to," I deadpanned.

Tommy's eyebrows lowered and he began to protest, but I threw a hand up to stop him. "I'm joking. As if!"

Tommy let out a huff. "Thank god. I was going to have to clip you both around the ears. What can I do for you?"

I briefly explained about Angela and the bucket list.

"Well now, that's better. I can draw you something up unless you have an idea of what you want?"

I looked at Saint George. I trusted Tommy's artistic ability. I told him as much.

He left us to go back to his work space and I sat beside Dallas as he flicked between the flash books. I tried not to think about how much this was going to hurt.

Blues music played through speakers in the corners of the room, the horns trying to compete with the thumping bass of torrential rain.

Tommy returned from the back, a pad and what looked like greaseproof paper in his hands. He passed both to me.

My hands flew to my mouth and I blinked back tears. It was perfect.

It was mostly black ink. A girl stood alone in the picture, her long dark hair blowing in the breeze and the skirt of her dress billowing around her feet. She was holding out a hand, and from it three large blue balloons had been released. I thought maybe she was yearning to get them back, but when I looked closer, she was smiling. She was letting them go.

Tommy cleared his throat. "It might be a little big for your first tattoo…"

"No, it's perfect. Absolutely perfect. Thank you, Tommy."

He scruffed my hair. "No problem, kid. Now come on back and we'll get it started."

THREE HOURS and forty-three minutes later, I was officially tattooed. The girl was just below my left shoulder, the balloons spread across my back by a strong wind. And goddamn it hurt. But eventually the steady, burning sting gave way to numbness, and I was able to do the whole thing in one sitting.

Tommy cleaned it up and wrapped it in cling wrap.

"Where's your bathroom? I've had to pee since the second balloon."

"Down the hall, to the left." I unfurled my back and walked stiffly down the hall.

I stood in the bathroom after I did my business, just staring at myself in the mirror, grinning like a fool. I hardly recognized the girl in the mirror, but she was a badass, with her blue hair and her awesome tattoo, although only one balloon poked out from under my shirt. I fluffed my hair and straightened my clothes.

I returned to the studio but stopped dead in the doorway. Dallas was shirtless and in the tattoo chair, and Tommy was tattooing the outline of a tiny blue balloon over his left pec. Over his heart.

Tears welled in my eyes. "Why?"

He smiled, that half grin that I loved so much. It is was touched with sadness. "You know why."

As the summer came to a close, so was our time together. Now we both had a permanent reminder of this one summer.

I swallowed back the lump in my throat and nodded. I stuffed the fear that I would never see Dallas again after my return to the "real world" to the back of my mind. This summer, hell the last two years even, was proof that unexpected things happened all the time. There was no reason to worry about the future if it meant you couldn't enjoy the present.

Tommy was unusually silent as he finished Dallas's balloon. He cleaned it up and gave him the same spiel about caring for your new ink that he gave me. He walked us back to the front of the shop and I pulled out my purse.

He just waved me away. "Don't worry about it. It's my gift to you and your friend. You're a good kid, Olivia."

I gave him a tight hug. "Thanks Tommy."

Dallas gave him another hug and we left, racing back to the car through the deluge.

I turned back to see Tommy still watching us through the plate glass window. I lifted my hand in a wave, and he gave me a sad smile and salute.

As we pulled into traffic, I couldn't get Tommy's sad face out of my head.

"Is Tommy married? Have kids?"

Dallas shook his head. "Nah. I heard my dad and Uncle Wyatt talking once. Dad and Tommy had been friends since they were kids, and Dad loved Tommy, but Tommy really loved Dad. Like love-love. When he joined the carnival, everyone knew, especially my mom. They became best friends, I guess because they both loved the same man. Tommy treated us like his own kids. But when my parents died, Tommy just left. Losing the great love of your life and your best friend at the same time had to hurt."

Probably not as much as losing both parents and a father-figure at once. Just one more loss for Dallas to bare at a time where he'd lost everything. It explained the look Tommy was giving us out the window too. It was longing, for the man who was Dallas' carbon copy.

I knew why Ruben and Dallas were such good men now. In an era where homophobia was rife, his dad loved the man in the only way he could. Made room for him in his life the only way he knew how.

I really wished I'd met Dallas's folks.

I thought of Frederick, and the fact there was now another sad parallel to my former life and the one I had now. Frederick had been shunned until he kept who he was a secret. Tommy had been given acceptance and love, but only a pale imitation of the love he desired.

Maybe after this summer was over, I could persuade Frederick to bring me to Odessa for a holiday, maybe stop in and visit my old acquaintance Tommy. Maybe convince Frederick to get a tattoo or something. Ha!

The lawyer and the tattoo artist. The thought made me smile.

CHAPTER FOURTEEN

LAS CRUCES, NEW MEXICO

Another afternoon thunderstorm rolled in, making a lot of noise, but not giving much relief from the pressing humidity. I was hungry and in all honesty, completely exhausted. I couldn't believe how much I had changed in a few short months. My skin was golden, and I'd gotten a small smattering of freckles across my nose from my time spent in the sun, despite my impressive collection of Hellson Brothers Carnival trucker caps. My hair had lightened three shades for the same reason, and every spare ounce of fat on my ass had melted away. I even had a pretty impressive set of biceps when I flexed.

But the continual roll-out of the carnival was starting to wear me down. I was an academic, dammit. I wasn't made for two a.m. long hauls and midnight teardowns. I was made for study halls and hot cups of tea. In less than two weeks, that would be my life. And despite my physical exhaustion, the thought of the summer ending made me want to cry.

The carnival had become so familiar to me now, like a home. The smells of dust, fries and humanity had become an old friend. The sounds of laughing teenagers, the whoosh of the Hurricane's hydraulics and the tinny organ music had become my favorite soundtrack. I would miss it, far more than the place I had lived for the past eighteen years.

I sighed as I walked back from my break, my heart as weary as my feet.

I stopped at the sound of a child crying. This wasn't an odd sound at a carnival. On average, I saw about thirty epic tantrums a day. But they weren't usually accompanied by a soul-rending sob. I walked down between two of the midway booths and saw a little boy sobbing on his knees. In front of him was a dead pigeon.

"Hey, are you okay?" Tears and dust made his face dirty, and I walked up to him slowly.

"The pigeon is dead," he hiccupped.

"Yeah it is. But it was probably of old age or something." I didn't know what to say to sad little boys. Where was Dallas when I needed him?

He looked up at me and swiped his sleeve across his cheeks. "You reckon?"

"Yeah I do." Well, it was either that or he was poisoned by pest control, but I'd keep that one to myself. "Where's your parents?"

The kid got to his feet. "Ma went to get me a hotdog. I played the clowns." He was probably about ten or eleven, and he had light brown hair but dark, straight eyebrows. There was something about the kid that just made him seem older, more serious than the kids who usually came around the carnival.

"How about we go find her? She's probably on her way back, but if she can't find you because you're hiding down here she might panic."

The kid gave me a solemn nod, and we walked out from between the booths.

"Dash!" A woman called, as if on cue, and the kid turned toward a blonde woman who was balancing two hotdogs and a soda in her hands.

"He's here," I called, and waved her over.

"Dash, baby, what's wrong?" She gave me a quick suspicious look, as if I had hurt her baby. Carnies, right?

"There's a dead bird, Ma. Right over there. I tried to do CPR, but it wouldn't wake up."

I grimaced at the thought of the kid putting his mouth anywhere near the pigeon. Ick.

"I heard him…" the kid gave me a sharp look, as if he didn't want me to tell his mother he was crying, "err, in distress, so I went to see what was wrong."

His mother's face folded itself into a look of forced happiness, but the traces of sadness didn't leave her eyes.

"It probably just died of old age, sweetie. There's nothing you could have done." She gave him a tight hug. "Now take your hot dog and soda over to the bench and have your lunch."

The kid took one of the offered hot dogs, and walked over to a park bench that was in desperate need of a coat of paint.

Dash's mother turned to me. "Sorry about that. His dog was just hit by a car, and his Daddy was in Afghanistan," her voice hitched a little on the word 'was'. "Now, he's determined to be a hero like his daddy, but with Fred the Dog's death, he's taking it hard. Even though we have a whole farm of rescued animals." She gave a choked laugh. I wanted to hug her, or turn back time, or rage about the injustices of life. After all, it was a rant I'd practiced many times.

Instead, I had a different idea.

"I might know just the thing…" And I set about explaining.

· · ·

"Are you sure you're ready for this?"

No. No I wasn't. But I knew this was the right thing to do. It reminded me of Dallas's kismet theory. Everything happening for a reason. Whatever, it was the right thing to do.

"I'm sure. This is the perfect solution. It's just hard, you know?"

He leaned across the cab of the truck and kissed my temple. "You are one amazing person."

I turned my head and kissed his lips lightly. "I bet you say that to all the girls."

"Only to you." He kissed my nose and jumped out of the truck. I took a deep breath, and climbed out too, leaning in to grab the box in the foot well. Dallas grabbed the bags of supplies that we picked up yesterday.

Turning, I let out a screech as I nearly ran into a giant pig. Its squinty little eyes stared at the box.

"Holy shit, you're huge!"

"Mama says you shouldn't say the S word," a small voice said from behind me. "Or blasflame. Busflame, umm…" Dash's nose scrunched up as he thought hard.

"Blaspheme, sweetie," Dash's mother, Tori, came up and rested her hand on the boys shoulder. "Take Prosciutto back to the barn and lock her away before she crash tackles these poor people for their groceries."

Dash whistled and took off running towards the barn. The giant pig, that must have weighed at least 100 times more than the kid, trotted behind him. As I watched, they were joined by two small goats, a group of chickens and a goose on their voyage to the barn.

"The pig thinks it's a dog. We raised it from days old. Actually, nearly everything thinks it's a dog on this place, except the dog. Fred thought he was a human." Tori gave me a warm smile. She reached out and shook Dallas's hand. "I'm Tori, by the way. You must be Dallas. Olivia told me all about you."

"Pleasures all mine, ma'am."

"Are you sure you want to do this? It's okay if you've changed your mind. I haven't mentioned it to Dash," she asked, and I shook my head and blinked back the water in my eyes.

Tori led us up over the porch. "Mind the hole. That board rotted last spring and I haven't had time to get someone out here to replace it." Their house was a small ranch house, the porch hugging it on three sides. The driveway had been a good half mile long, and the mountains loomed over the flat, dry plains like guardians.

She led us through a screen door that squeaked,

and into a sitting room. It reminded me of Angela's house when we were young. There was always a pile of folded clothes on the recliner, and several toys scattered across a worn round mat, but it just added to the homeliness of the place. However, unlike Angela's house, there was a tortoise walking the halls with a red helium balloon tied around his shell.

"Don't mind Spartacus. We lost him once, found him halfway down the drive. They may be slow, but they can really hide." Tori gave the tortoise one of the raspberries that sat on a bowl on the counter. The little tortoise gobbled it down like it was the heart of his enemy, bits of berry smeared over its beak. I was totally in love.

"I can fix that board, if you have the materials?" Dallas offered casually. Tori looked like she was going to refuse, and I recognized that prideful look. I had it too.

"Let him. He needs something to do with his hands. He doesn't know how to sit still."

Tori sighed. "There should be something out in the barn. Dash will show you where it is."

Dallas gave her his one hundred watt smile and walked back out the screen door, letting it close softly behind him.

"He reminds me of my husband. Gives you that

grin and before you know it, you're agreeing to something that your mamma wouldn't approve of."

Wasn't that the truth!

"Come on, we'll get a coffee. I made tollhouse cookies as well. They're Dash's favorite."

Dash came tearing into the house as if he had some special cookie radar.

"Did you show Mister Dallas where the boards were?" Tori asked, smacking his fingers away from the plate of cookies. "Uh! Wash your hands first. And get that pout off your face, Miss Olivia has brought you something."

Dash lived up to his name, as he was in the washroom and back before I could blink. He eyed me and then the box.

Dallas came back through the door and came to stand behind me. I lowered the box to the floor and peeled back the lid. Inside, three tiny kittens slept.

"Oh wow! Mama, there's kittens in the box, and they are so small, oh look one's waking up! Can I hold it? Why are they so little?"

Catticus reached its little paws up the side of the box, and let out a pitiful mew noise.

They were so cute when they were asleep. I cleared my throat. "They're small because they are really young. Six weeks to be exact. Too young to be away from their mother. But the Mama cat had an accident, so I've been raising these little guys since they were a week old." The boy picked up the kitten with gentle hands, way too gentle for a boy his age, and I knew then that I'd made the right choice.

"But they are getting too big to be cooped up in my trailer all the time, so I need someone to finish raising them. Someone grown up and brave, because loving something is hard but loving something so helpless is even harder."

"And there's three of them, so the person'd have to be extra brave."

"That's right. So I was wondering if you would look after them for me? It'd be a lot of work, and you'd have to do it because your mom has enough on her plate. You think you could do it? But be sure."

The kitten took to the boy like they'd been friends forever. He curled up on his chest, paws kneading Dash's chest. Dash considered my words.

"They'd like it here. There's plenty of mice to catch in the barn." He thought harder, his brows hanging low over his eyes. "I can do it. I'll take good care of them, I promise."

The other two kittens woke up and wanted out of the box too. I handed JK to Tori and put Catsby on my own lap. "I know you will, Dash. Thanks."

"Won't you miss them, though?" I petted the soft ball of fluff on my lap, feeling its tiny purr vibrating against my thigh. I would miss them a lot. Their kitten antics, and their warm weights on my chest at night, and the way I was never alone even in the darkest hours. But Dash needed the kittens as much as they needed him.

"I'll miss them a lot, and I'll be sad for a while, but I'll know deep down that the kittens are happy here with you. They are somewhere better."

"Like Daddy? And Fred the Dog?"

Oh god. *Do not cry. Do not cry. Do not cry.*

Still my voice came out a little rougher. "Yeah, though I'm sure you're Dad and Fred are somewhere even happier."

Dallas cleared his throat. "I better go start on the porch." He hightailed it out of there as if he were on fire, but not before I saw the shine in his eyes. I should have thought that Dash's loss might hit a little too close to his own story. Stupid Olivia.

I straightened my shoulders. "Why don't you go play with the kittens, let them get used to you. In one of those bags, there's some cat toys and a few treats." Dash plopped Catticus over his shoulder, and I placed Catsby on the other. He gently cradled JK in his arms, as she had always been the smallest.

Tori and I watched in silence as the boy and the kittens bonded, laughing at the crazy kitten antics and Dash's childish giggles. I could hear Dallas hammering away at the porch, and we made small talk. Tori was a Las Cruces native, and had spent her whole life on this very ranch. Good investments and a widow's pension meant she could raise Dash there too. But they only scraped by.

"You sure three extra mouths won't be too much?"

Dash let out another giggle as JK tackled Catsby. "It's fine. The animals make him so happy, and they give me a little solace too, if I'm honest. Every dollar is worth it to see him smile."

The front door opened and a slightly sweaty Dallas walked in the door. His hair was tousled and his cheeks had a touch of red, but damn if he wasn't the sexiest thing I'd ever seen.

"As a woman who's been in your position, you are in so much trouble," Tori whisper-laughed at me.

He gave us a satisfied grin. "All done. Should last another fifty years."

"It might be the last plank standing, but thank you so much. Both of you."

Dallas threw a quick look at where Dash was playing on the floor. "You're more than welcome, ma'am."

"Pssh, it's Tori. None of this ma'am business. Would you two like to stay for lunch?"

I shook my head and stood. "Thanks for the offer,

but we better hit the road. We have to get to Surprise by morning, and still have to pack up our gear."

I walked over to where Dash was playing with my babies. I picked up each one, and rubbed my face on their soft fur. "Behave yourselves, okay? Be good for Dash."

I put them back in the box and walked out the door, suddenly desperate to leave so I could have a sniffle in private.

Tori walked us back to the truck, and thankfully Prosciutto was nowhere in sight.

I gave her Frederick's card. "If you ever need anything, Frederick will know where to find me."

Tori wrapped me in a hug, squeezing me tightly, then gave Dallas one too.

"You guys stop in next summer when the carnival comes back to town, you hear? Or if you ever just happen to be close by. You are always welcome in my home."

I could only nod. I wouldn't be with the carnival next year.

I jumped in the car and closed the door. Dash was on the porch with one of the kittens, and I gave him a wave. He gently cradled the kitten, I couldn't tell which from in the truck, in one hand and waved with the other.

"Oh, by the way, I put a couple of hundred bucks for their spaying in the carton of wet food."

"You didn't have to do that!" Tori shook her head.

"Yes we did! Take good care of them."

I gave them another wave as we passed them on the way back down the drive.

"This is a good thing, you know, even though it hurts." Dallas reached over and squeezed my hand as we bumped down the drive.

"It had to happen. At least it was a happy ending."

The more painful ending was still to come.

CHAPTER FIFTEEN

I snuggled back into Dallas's arms and watched the fire in barrel flicker and splutter. The sound of laughter and friendship drowned out the sounds of the freeway. I smiled as Dallas's chest rumbled against my cheek as he laughed at something Manny said. I wasn't really paying attention, just soaking the feeling of contentment into my bones.

We were having a last night blow out. Most of the itinerant workers would branch off now, heading off to wherever their lives were lived during the other nine months of the year. Baba cooked up the remaining perishable ingredients into an end of season feast fit for kings, instead of us lowly carnies, the gypsies of the twenty-first century.

I wasn't worried; I still had at least a week with

my surrogate family. A skeleton crew would take the carnival to its winter home, a massive warehouse where everything would be washed, scrubbed and all the mechanical parts eyeballed and maintained until they were basically new. That would happen over autumn.

Elise told me that she and Wyatt spent winter and spring in semi-retirement. They had a little love shack down in Santa Cruz, and they spent the cooler months visiting their kids and playing golf and fishing. Come spring, they'd move to the big house that Ruben owned in Pensacola, and they'd go to work ensuring that the Carnival was ready for the summer months.

Baba and Ted visited their kids in Canada over the off season, and I'd been surprised to hear that they even had kids. They hadn't said a single word about them the whole season. Well, that wasn't very surprising for Ted, but Baba and I had talked a lot. I guess everyone had been caught up in my drama, and then Liz's drama, then my drama again. Manny and Dallas did construction during winter, and Ruben made furniture out of his garage.

I felt like that my friends, my family, had alter egos that I had no idea about. Like a traveling salesman with three families, all in different states.

"How'd your friend's list go, Livvy?" Elise asked.

"I did thirteen of the things. I think she would have been happy with that. She would have loved the carnival, and all of you guys. I can't thank you enough for your help." Thinking of Angela no longer made my chest ache under the crushing grief. She'd be happy about that too.

I'm proud of you, Livvy, she would have said. *I knew in there was a fierce, independent badass waiting to get out. I saw you. I knew she was there. I loved you both.*

"Oh, Honey, you don't need to thank us for anything. It's been a wild ride, but I'm glad we were here to share it with you."

I reached over and squeezed her hand.

"Nothing's ever boring when Livvy's around," Dallas said, kissing the top of my head.

"I'll have you know, I used to be super boring. You're a bad influence. I'll probably go back to being super boring when I'm in college. All textbooks and study groups."

"You'll never be boring to me," he whispered and kissed my cheek.

"Get a room, Lovebirds. There's a baby present." Ruben pointed to the dozing Iris in Ida's arms. Ida and Iris would live in Pensacola with Ruben and Dallas. No one had any idea if Liz would return once the carnival season was over, and although Elise's daughter sent updates on Liz's wellbeing, no one was any wiser as to what the future held.

"As you command, Big Bro. Come on, Livvy." Ruben rolled his eyes, but he was smirking. I'm pretty sure he thought we were bumping uglies, but he'd be wrong. Despite countless opportunities, we had yet to get pass second base. Or maybe it was the dugout. I thought of all the nights we lie pressed together in my trailer, long kisses and roaming hands. Nope, we had definitely gotten to first base.

Dallas led me out of the firelight, and towards my van. Maybe tonight would be it. My heart began to thunder, and my toes started to tingle.

But instead of heading toward my trailer, Dallas stopped at his truck. Disappointment flowed through me, dousing the flames of lust. I climbed into the passenger seat.

"Where are we going now?"

"Surely you know me by now, Liv. It's a surprise."

I laughed. "A surprise in Surprise. That's corny, even for you." But secretly, I was touched.

"I know you love it. Don't pretend." Apparently he knew me too. I did love it. Almost as much as I loved him.

"It's a bit of a drive. Why don't you have a nap?" It was only 9pm, but I'd never made a good passenger. It's like I became a narcoleptic or something.

I watched the white lines within the glow of the headlights, and it put me out quicker than a hypnotists pocket watch.

A LIGHT KISS on my lips woke me. "Hey, Sleeping Beauty. We are here."

I blinked at his beautiful face leaning over mine in the red neon light. I gave him a sleepy smile.

Neon.

I bolted upright. Holy shit. Holy shit. We were in Vegas. Las-freaking-Vegas.

In the front of a small white wedding chapel. Dallas handed me Angela's open journal, a ring resting on its pages.

"Number ten; get married in Vegas by Elvis. Olivia Jefferson, will you marry me? Just for tonight?"

The ring was a deep blue Lapis Lazuli, its light silver flecks flashing in the neon glow.

In all honesty, I couldn't tell you what went through my head in that moment. Looking back, it was all just white noise. Static.

But my heart knew. My head was nodding and I was saying yes before my brain even caught up. *Relax, Olivia, it's for a night, not forever.* The disappointment I felt at that thought was completely insane.

Dallas's smile threatened to blind me. "Woo! Let's go get hitched."

He was around to my door in seconds. He held out a hand, and helped me down, pressing me close to his body. He kissed me like it was the first time we'd kissed. With all the passion and potential two crazy kids could possess.

I looked down at my jeans, and one of Dallas check shirts thrown over a Hellson Brothers polo.

"You look beautiful, and I would happily marry you even if you were wearing a sack. But I figured a girl has to have a wedding dress."

He reached behind my seat and pulled out a large rectangle box, the name of a boutique embossed on the front.

"How long have you been planning this for?" I asked, as he reached back behind the passenger seat and pulled out my purse and my beauty case.

"Since Nuevo Laredo. That's where I got the ring."

"And the dress?"

"At a little boutique in Odessa. Tommy told me where it was. He helped me pick it, too. Now we better hurry if we are going to make our ceremony."

"Dallas, it's 12:30 at night!"

He tucked the dress box under one arm, and pulled me close with the other. "This is Vegas, baby. We can get married any time. Besides, I knew we'd have to do this at night, otherwise you'd rationalize the hell out of it in the light of day. Let's not think about it. Let's just do this one wild thing."

I kissed his chin. "You are crazy, Dallas Hellson."

"Crazy about you, soon-to-be Mrs. Hellson."

He wrapped an arm around my shoulders, and we walked into the little white chapel, with its Vegas style neon sign bathing us in a warm glow. Dallas pointed me towards a women's restroom just inside the doors.

"Go change, I'll talk to the people at reception." Another quick kiss to my lips.

"Are you sure about this, Dallas? You know, you don't have to marry me to take my virginity," I joked.

"I know that, but I find that I kind of like the idea of being your husband the first time."

I blushed right down to my toes, and the heat curled low in my abdomen again. Tonight was definitely the night. I didn't believe in Jesus, but he'd be glad that I wasn't going to do it out of wedlock. Though I don't think Elvis was the conduit that the Holy Son had in mind.

I pushed through the white door to the bathrooms, its picture of a bride covered in rhinestones making me giggle. I rested the dress box on top of the large marble sink, sliding the lid from the top.

Easing the dress from its bed of tissue paper, I swallowed a rather large lump in my throat. It was a soft gauzy fabric, in an empire cut. The bodice had a halter neckline, trimmed in gold lace, the same as the band that cinched the bodice just under my bust. The hem also had the same ornate gold trim where it brushed the floor. It was simple, and beautiful. Perfect. The bodice had built in support, so I shucked all my clothes but my underwear, and breathed a sigh of relief that I wore my boring white cotton panties today. I quickly pulled the dress up over my hips, and fastened the hooks at the back of my neck. I left my bra on the floor, the built in support in the dress would have to do for the night.

I let out my hair from its messy bun, and brushed and moussed it until it fell in soft waves around my face. Three coats of mascara, and some red lipstick later, I was ready to get married. I took off my work boots and put them in a plastic shopping bag someone had stuffed in the trash can. I didn't have any shoes worthy of the dress, so I was going to have to meet my groom barefoot.

As I exited the restroom, a woman in her late forties met me at the door. "Olivia?"

"Yes?"

"You look wonderful. Here, let me take your things. I'll keep them in the cloak room until you're done. Your groom is waiting for you at the altar, but first, let's get some paperwork out of the road." She took the box and the shopping bag from my hands, and led me to the reception desk.

"I'll just get you to sign the consent form, saying you are willing to undergo this marriage, and the prenuptial agreement, here. Just sign where the sticky arrows are. The groom has already signed."

"A prenup?"

"Just standard. We give them to all our newly-weds, unless they sign the waiver. Despite the saying, not everything stays in Vegas."

I quickly read through the agreement, noting that it was pretty standard terms. Each of would retain all premarital assets and split anything earned during the marriage. I signed, and tried not to imagine what my father, or Frederick, would say right now.

"All done? Okay, one more little surprise from the groom." She opened the fridge and pulled out a flower garland made of white roses and daisies. "This one is for here," she reached up and placed it on my head before reaching back into the little bar fridge and pulling out a posy of yellow and white roses. "Every bride needs a bouquet. Now you are set. Come this way."

She led me further into the chapel, past a set of double doors.

She signaled a guy who looked like he should be playing in a blues club instead of a Vegas wedding chapel. He was dressed all in black, down to the black raybans and a fedora. He started banging out *Here Comes the Bride* on an ancient looking organ.

"Off you go, Lovie. It's time." The receptionist gave me a little shove, and I looked down the aisle.

Dallas had changed into a white dress shirt, and tight black jeans that looked new. A pair of black suspenders ran up over his torso. A gold bowtie finished off his outfit. He looked amazing.

I couldn't help the grin on my face as I walked down the aisle slowly. Left foot forward, feet together. Right foot forward, feet together. Repeat. Until I was standing in front of him, looking up into his sparkling eyes. The look he gave me made me feel breathless.

"You look so... I don't know. Beautiful just doesn't seem enough. You are a goddess."

My cheeks heated with pleasure. I held both of his hands in mine. "You too."

"Uh, huh. Dearly Beloveds..." I hadn't noticed Elvis until he spoke, but I wasn't sure how I missed him. He was more bejeweled then a fifth grader's backpack. He was full Vegas Elvis too; white jumpsuit with silver rhinestones, a slight paunch and killer sideburns. He even had the Elvis lip curl.

"We are here today to marry Dallas Thomas Hellson and Olivia…"

"Francis."

"Olivia Francis Jefferson, in holy matrimony. Marriage, like classic rock'n'roll, lasts a lifetime. It is an institution to be respected, and cherished, until the end of time.

"Olivia, do you take Dallas to be your lawful wedded husband?"

I swallowed hard. "I do."

"And Dallas, do you take Olivia to be your lawful wedded wife?"

"I do." Not even a hint of hesitation in his voice.

"Well, now. May your love be tender, and may your love be true. By the powers vested in me by the one true King of Rock'n'Roll and by the State of Nevada, I now pronounce you husband and wife, uh-huh yeah. You may kiss your bride."

Dallas swept me into his arms, and branded me with a kiss. His lips moved against mine, his tongue running along my lower lip. He lifted his head just before the kiss got positively indecent for a public place.

The witnesses, two strangers who I'd never met, threw confetti at us as we walked back down the aisle. I laughed when I realized they were shaped like tiny doves. This was the most amazing night of my life. Even if it was a fantasy.

We signed the marriage certificates, and they took photos of us with Elvis, and some without. They printed them on the spot, putting them inside a folder with the words I GOT MARRIED BY ELVIS in big gold letters.

I thanked the lady at the desk as she got my stuff. "One second," Dallas said, as he scooped me up and strode out of the chapel. "Barefoot goddess," he murmured, kissing my lips as he strode to his truck. Unclipping the door with his fingers, he pushed the door open. "Beautiful wife." He kissed me again, full of heat and promises.

He raced back to the chapel and collected my things, putting them in the lockbox on the back of his truck. I looked at the dash clock and realized it was nearly two a.m. He climbed in next to me, that ridiculous, satisfied grin still on his face. I knew what that face meant. There were more surprises to come.

We pulled up at the valet parking section of the Bellagio. "We can't afford this!"

"Look at you, using the royal 'we' already.

Married life suits you. Don't worry, it was all part of the package." He came around and lifted me out of the truck, carrying me to the carpeted entrance. He got a large black duffle from the lock box on the back of his truck and handed the keys to the valet.

Hand in hand, we walked into one of the fanciest hotels in Vegas. And I wasn't even wearing shoes.

CHAPTER SIXTEEN

LAS VEGAS, NEVADA

My stomach felt like it was filled with a million butterflies as we stood in front of a door to room 608. No, butterflies was too mild, maybe bald eagles.

My heart raced, and I got more and more nervous as each second passed. "Let's go in."

Dallas dropped his duffle beside the door and swiped the key card. He pushed the door open until it locked into place. He threw the duffle into the darkness of the room.

"You look a little pale, Liv. You know we can just go in there, order room service ice-cream and watch infomercials, right? There's no pressure."

I leaned in, pressing the full length of my body against his, my head tilting back for a kiss.

"I know. I've been waiting for this for weeks. I'm just a little nervous is all."

He leaned in, dropping a soft kiss on my lips. Then he picked me up, our lips still touching, and I wrapped my arms and legs around his body as he strode across the threshold.

Pressing me against the wall as he kicked the door shut, he deepened the kiss. I kissed him back with all the pent up heat I felt coursing through my blood, my body wiggling against the hardness in his jeans.

He let out a long groan. He moved us towards the bed. He stepped around his bag, but caught his left foot on the strap

For a second, we both launched through the air as he tripped, but the room was tiny and I landed with a whooshed breath on the bed, Dallas's weight on top of me expelling all the air from my lungs.

"That was way smoother in my head," Dallas said from on top of me, and I began to giggle. My giggle graduated to a laugh, and then it spiraled out of control until I was curled in a ball, my stomach aching and Dallas was laughing right along with me.

"I have to pee," I gasped out, getting my breath back. I shifted off the bed and walked into the bathroom.

I cleaned myself up a little, and then looked at the

bride in the mirror. Thank goodness my mascara was waterproof, or Dallas would be making love to Alice Cooper right now.

When I left the bathroom, my previous nerves were gone. Dallas had turned on one of the table lamps, bathing the room in a soft glow. He sat on the end of the bed, just waiting for me. I walked toward him, my hips swaying, feeling like the goddess he told me I was.

Dallas's eyes were hooded and his lips formed a small O as his gaze tracked me like a predator. He stood, unbuttoning his shirt. He'd lost his tie and suspenders at some point already.

As my eyes took in the hard planes of his chest, the light dusting of hair trailing down his abs to where his jeans looked uncomfortably tight, I realized my nerves had been replaced with hunger.

I trailed a hand down the front of his torso, and he let out a little hiss. My other hand joined the first, and I explored his chest, his abs, the V of his hips. He stood there, body tense and chest heaving as he let me explore at my own pace.

I reached behind my neck to unhook my dress, but Dallas caught my hands. "Let me."

He unhooked the fastenings at the back, and I stood there, my hands still on his chest, as the dress slid down my body on a whisper until it pooled at my feet.

Dallas let out a hard breath as if he'd been punched. "God, you are so perfect."

My hands went to the button of his jeans, and I popped it open, pushing them down his hips with awkward hands. His dick sprang free, and I reached out to stroke it, marveling at both the heat and the hardness.

Dallas put his hand over mine. "If you do that, I won't last thirty seconds." He moved my hand back up to his neck and he put his hands on my hips, pulling me close until we were skin to skin. "Dammit, I mightn't last thirty seconds anyway. So beautiful." His hands ran over my hips and ass like he was committing them to memory.

He turned us, lying me down on the bed and pressing his big body along mine. Then he kissed me, hot and hard until our tongues danced to the same rhythm of our wandering hands.

When he broke the kiss, he was grinning. "I'm going to make you feel so good, you won't even remember your own name. This is going to be perfect, I promise." He started trailing kisses down my body and my brain went on hiatus.

But Dallas definitely kept his promise. Olivia who?

. . .

BRIGHT SUNLIGHT BURNED through the window, waking me. I stretched and smiled at the languid ache of my body. I looked over at Dallas, still asleep on his stomach in bed beside me, the white sheet only covering his bottom half. I couldn't help but run my fingers over the curve of his back. He was a sculptor's dream. One blue eye slid open, and a lazy smile curled his lips.

"Good morning, Beautiful. How are you feeling?" His hand snaked out to my waist, his thumb stroking my ribs. I pressed my body close to his.

"A bit achy. But if I felt any happier, I might explode."

"Me too. How about I go fill the Jacuzzi and you order whatever breakfast you want from room service?"

I'd forgotten the big black tub I'd seen in the bathroom last night. I shifted out of the bed and walked to the bathroom, where fresh robes hung on hooks. I slipped one over my naked body. Walking back into the bedroom, I couldn't help the powerful feeling in my body at the look on Dallas's face. He was hungry, but it wasn't for pancakes.

"Change of plans. Come back to bed."

I didn't need to be asked twice.

Two hours later, I answered the door to room service. Dallas was on the phone to Ruben while the Jacuzzi was filling.

"Yeah, I'll meet you guys there. Thank Elise for us."

Us. Didn't that just make me all fuzzy on the inside.

"Did you tell Ruben that we were getting hitched?"

Dallas nearly choked on his pancake. "Hell no. Can you imagine? He'd have had a coronary if he knew. Maybe we'll tell him when we get it annulled. Not like he can murder me then."

I laughed, but I was a little sad at the thought of the annulment. Not that I didn't want it, because I was way too young to be married and everything was so uncertain. But I was enjoying our little fantastical wedded bliss for the while.

Dallas wrapped his arms around my waist and sat me on his lap, his robe gaping open to show a good view of his muscular thighs. Mmm.

"Are you ready for surprise number three?"

I raised my eyebrows. "I thought surprise number three was that thing you did with your tongue last night."

He chuckled, leaning over to give me a quick

kiss. "Okay, surprise number four. We have this room for the rest of the week."

I pulled back, so I could see if he was joking or not. "We can't afford this for a whole week."

"Sure I can. Besides, number thirteen states you had to spend a week in the sun. This is your week. Relax, take some time before school."

"Why do I detect a but?"

His hand skimmed down my back to knead the swell of my ass.

"I can detect a butt too."

"Dallas!" I rolled my eyes at his corny joke.

"But, I have to go back to LA today and help unload. Ruben can't spare the hands. Then I can race back here. I'll be back the day after next at the latest. Then we'll spend the rest of the time drinking mojitos in the sun, and then we'll fill out the annulment details on the way out of town. I like the idea of you being Mrs. Dallas Hellson for a little longer."

I leaned over and bit the tip of his chin. "Don't you mean Mrs. Jefferson-Hellson."

He cupped my cheeks. "Whatever you want. I'll even be Dallas Jefferson if that's what makes you happy." He fed me a strawberry, and I sucked his finger into my mouth like they do in the movies. Let me tell you, the movies didn't lie about the effects of that little maneuver either. I was on my back on the bed and being kissed like I was the only source of oxygen in outer space before I could even think of a reply.

Twice on the bed and once in the Jacuzzi later, Dallas was kissing me goodbye at the door. I fell into the thousand thread count sheets and slept for twelve hours.

DALLAS HAD PACKED my bag the way a horny teenage boy would. Every pair of lacy panties I owned was in there, along with my bikini. He'd packed most of my dresses, but only one t-shirt, and the only pair of jeans I had were the dirty ones I came in. No PJ's or socks, but at least I had my boots and my ballet flats. In the bag was a jumbo box of condoms. He'd left me his phone, and I made a note to buy my own.

It had suited me to be unreachable after my parents had cancelled my phone contract, but now I was heading to college, and away from Dallas, I needed another ASAP.

The weather was overcast, and I looked through Angela's bucket list. The journal was fat now, filled with photos and mementos of my time in the carnival, little notes and tidbits I'd picked up along the way. Dallas had drawn little caricatures of us, which were surprisingly good. He had a real artistic talent.

I loved the one of us getting our naked butts chased by the alligator. But my favorite photo was still of me and Dallas silhouetted by the lights of the Hurricane.

There was only one thing left on the list, and happily, it was an easy one. I pocketed the key card into my purse, and made sure I looked okay. Did I look different now I'd been, as Angela would have said, deflowered? I'd teased her that she sounded like a 1950s housewife, but she decided it sounded more poetic than "losing your virginity." She was such a drama queen sometimes. Despite the silly grin and the loose feeling in my limbs, I still looked like Olivia to me. But the new Olivia. The survivor. The badass.

Walking out the front doors of the Bellagio, I smiled and tipped the doorman.

"Thank you, Miss."

"You're very welcome..." I squinted at his nametag, "Steven. You have a good day."

Steve the doorman smiled. "I believe that's my line, Miss. Can I get you a cab?"

"No thanks, Steve. But you can tell me where I could find..." I leaned in close and whispered my destination in his ear.

"Oh! Well, I do believe there is one in the Miracle Mile shops. Across the road and down a block."

I tipped my imaginary hat. "Thanks Steve!" I yelled over my shoulder as I walked down past the Bellagio fountains.

The guy at the crosswalk was wearing a yellow and cornflower blue paisley that would have been cutting edge fashion in the seventies, but still nice now.

"Hey, I like your tie."

The guy looked at the offending article. "Thanks. It's my lucky tie. My ex-wife hated it, so I wore it to all our divorce proceedings," his voice was hoarse from way too much whiskey and cigarettes, and he wheezed out a laugh.

"Uh, great. Well, good luck in Vegas." Awkward.

The rain was holding out, and I was feeling upbeat as I walked through the Miracle Mile mall. Finding the shop I wanted, I strolled through the doors like I belonged there.

Number twelve; buy Victoria's Secret lingerie.

"Hi there. You just give me holla if you need some help," the shop assistant said perkily before going back to her phone.

So. Much. Lingerie. I really needed my best friend for this one. I picked up a red set.

You heard Great Aunt Eustace, Livvy. Red is only for pirates and prostitutes. But given the fact you're wearing it for your husband, I'm going with pirate.

I flicked through the racks as Angela's voice ran commentary in my brain. *Too virginal. Too Mrs. Robinson. Too black.*

I stopped at a deep green set. The bra was a cute demi-cup and the briefs were a soft silk in a French cut. They had black ribbon crisscrossing up the sides. All it would take is one small tug and they'd disappear.

I took it and the red set into the change rooms. "I'd just like to try these on?"

"Go for it, Honey. But remember, underwear goes on the outside like Superman 'til you bought it." Her voice was slightly Midwestern, so she must have been a recent transplant to Vegas. "Remember, it should cup the girls gently, not smoosh them out like sausage meat."

Well, that was a visual I didn't need. I tried on both sets.

I eyed the price tag. I definitely couldn't afford both. I couldn't get Great Aunt Eustace's voice out of my head, so I went with the green.

It lifted and cupped like a dream. Looking in the full length mirror I appreciated just how hot I appeared. Everything was firmer from all my manual labor, and my arms and legs were golden. You could still use my stomach as a replacement lighthouse beacon it was so pale, but it was flat and if

I sucked in my belly enough, I got a really awesome two pack.

Dallas was lucky to have me. I was a catch! He was going to swallow his tongue when he saw me in this, though. He called me last night to let me know he'd gotten back to LA safely, and the dirty things he told me he wanted to do to me over the phone still made my cheeks blush and heat pool down south.

I quickly paid for my lingerie and left. As I walked back to the hotel, the clouds finally shifted and the sun came out. About time.

I was going to hit the poolside.

So this was the life of the rich and famous. Well, I guess technically I had been rich, but my parents would never have approved of such wasteful and unsavory pastimes like drinking five dollar water because it came with cucumber wheels and a slice of lime in it. Or lying by the pool making no contribution to humanity whatsoever.

I, on the other hand, adored it.

The sun's rays bit into my shoulders, rapidly drying the dampness from my skin. If reincarnation was real, I was coming back as a seal.

Dallas's phone rang and I rolled over to answer it. Ruben's number displayed on the screen. Dallas had been using his brother's phone to text me updates. I couldn't wait to see him tomorrow. I missed him.

I swiped the phone to answer. "Hey Dallas, you'll never guess where I am."

"It's Ruben." His voice was serious. Oh shit, Dallas must have told him about the wedding. Shit. Shit.

"What's up, Ruben?" I tried for a calm and pacifying tone.

"Liv, there's been an accident."

I could pinpoint the moment my heart stopped beating, because I could no longer hear it thumping above the sound of blood rushing in my ears.

"What?"

"There was an accident unloading. Dallas was hurt." Ruben sounded… distraught. Level headed, unflappable Ruben.

"Is he okay?"

"He's alive. He's in surgery now. He had swelling on his brain so they are operating to relieve the pressure, but his lower half was crushed."

I just froze, like my body refused to follow the screaming demands of my mind to do something.

"Liv?"

And then, like someone else took possession of my body, I snapped into action.

"I'll be there in three hours. You tell him I'll be there. Keep me updated."

I grabbed the phone and my room key and sprinted into the hotel. I didn't care who I bumped, knocked or jostled.

I raced toward concierge desk. I skidded to a stop in front of an unflappable looking concierge.

"How can I help?"

"There's been an accident and I need to get to LA as soon as possible. I need to check out, and I need you to book me the next flight to LAX and I need a car there and I don't care if you have to buy First Class it needs to be the next flight!" It all came out in one garbled rush.

But the concierge was completely calm. "It'll be fine, ma'am. You go upstairs and pack your things, and by the time you get back down everything will be taken care of. I'll put everything on your credit card?"

Technically, it was Dallas's card, but I'd pay him back, because he was going to be fine. He could yell at me about it later.

I punched the elevator button repeatedly, willing it to hurry.

When I reached my room, I stuffed everything in the duffle without care. My brain kept circling back to Dallas, and Angela. It wouldn't end the same. Dallas was tougher than that.

Grabbing the phone charger from the wall on the way out the door, I didn't even stop and look back at the room that already held so many memories. I needed Dallas.

I skipped the elevator and raced down the stairs, skidding to a stop in front of the concierge. She handed me a large envelope.

"You are on the next flight out in thirty minutes. I've already checked you in, so go straight to the gate. I've called the airline and they know you are coming and that it's an emergency. Your boarding pass is in the envelope with your bill. The doorman is holding a cab for you out the front."

My eyes welled and a tear escaped to roll down my cheek.

"Thanks."

The concierge waved me away. "It's nothing. Now go. And good luck," she called out as I ran through the lobby.

Steve the Doorman was leaning through the window, talking to the cabbie. He straightened up and held the door open for me.

"I told the cabbie that you had to make this flight. He'll take care of you."

I threw him another watery smile. "Thanks Steve."

The cabbie peeled out of the lot like we were in a car chase. "It's thirteen minutes to the airport from here, but I can get you there in seven." He took the corner way too fast, but I didn't care. He could be going at light speed and it wouldn't be fast enough.

We ran three yellow lights and didn't go below sixty, but I was at the airport in exactly 7 minutes.

I handed the guy a fifty. "Thank you."

"Safe journey," he yelled through the open passenger window.

I raced through the security lines, pushing ahead and apologizing even though I didn't mean it. I got to the front and I prayed that neither my bags nor I beeped going through the X-ray's.

By some kind of holy providence, I got through without hassle. I ran up to the gate desk.

"Olivia Jefferson?" the desk attendant asked. I nodded furiously. "Come on through, the plane departs in five minutes."

She led me down the walkway and into first class, where she handed me off to the flight attendant.

The attendant stowed my bag in the overhead lockers and I strapped myself in. The flight attendant came back with a small bottle of brandy. It was just then I realized how much of a wreck I must have looked.

"Just breathe," she said, as the Captain's voice came overhead, telling everyone to prepare themselves for takeoff.

I downed the brandy in one go, and picked up the phone that was nestled in the armrest beside me.

"Frederick? It's Olivia. I need your help."

CHAPTER SEVENTEEN

RONALD REAGAN UCLA MEDICAL CENTER

"Dallas Hellson. I'm here to see Dallas Hellson. The reception said he was in ICU.

"I'm sorry, Miss, but its family only."

"I understand that. I am family."

"Are you his sister?"

"No, I'm his wife!" It came out louder than I expected, the word wife echoing off the stark white walls.

A curtain opened, and Ruben stuck his head out. "His what?"

Wyatt came out from behind the curtain. "It's okay, she can take my place. I need to get some coffee anyhow." He came over and took my bag, giving my hand a tight squeeze.

"He'll be okay. He looks rough, but we breed them tough."

I nodded and my eyes welled again. They were already red raw.

I walked in, and had to choke down a sob. Dallas looked like a broken doll. His head was bandaged up, and a tube running down his throat was attached to a machine that clicked in the corner. I grabbed his hand and kissed it.

"Talk to me, Ruben. What the fuck happened?"

Ruben slumped down into the hard plastic chair beside the bed. "The cross poles for the carousel hadn't be secured down tightly enough. Rubbed against strap holding it on the way home in until it gave out suddenly when we were unloading. The beams rolled off and hit him. Fractured his legs in eleven places. It was divine intervention that it didn't crush his torso too. He wouldn't be here right now if it had. As it is, he fell back and cracked his head on the concrete. His brain swelled and they had to do emergency surgery to relieve the pressure. He's in an induced coma for five days until the swelling goes down. They're waiting for an orthopedic surgeon to fix his legs."

As we spoke, the doctor came in. He checked Dallas's chart. "We are just waiting on an orthopedic surgeon. There was a minor bus crash in Glendale. Lots of broken bones."

"I want the best surgeon on the West Coast operating on Dallas as soon as possible. I don't care how much it costs."

I'm sure the doctor didn't realize he was doing it, but he looked me over, and then Ruben. No doubt taking in my Target purchased wardrobe and Ruben's torn and dirty jeans.

"Don't look at him. Look at me. Trust me when I say I have more money than god, and get me the best surgeon available ASAP." I must have channeled something of my father in that moment, because the doctor just gave a tight nod.

"I'll make some phone calls."

Once he left, Ruben raised an eyebrow at me. "I don't pay you that well."

I walked over to the other side of Dallas's bed, and entwined my fingers in his.

"Trust fund Princess, remember?"

"I thought you were a Hellson now?"

"Temporarily."

We sat in silence, just watching Dallas's chest rise and fall, irrevocable proof that he was still alive. That he hadn't left me just yet.

. . .

THE MORPHINE STARTED to wear off about half an hour later and Dallas's face creased in pain. I was about to ask the nurse for more when a young man, no more than thirty-five walked in. He was dressed in a light blue shirt with the sleeves rolled up, and grey suit pants. Both had been tailored to fit his body perfectly. He had the body of a gym junkie.

"I'm Jake Thorne, orthopedic surgeon." He pulled back Dallas's sheet, and probed his legs with gentle but sure fingers. When he touched Dallas foot, he frowned a little.

"You look a little young to be the best orthopedic surgeon on the West Coast." Even Angela would have been horrified at my rudeness.

"And you look a little young to be someone's wife, but looks can be deceiving. You asked for the best, and here I am, despite being twelve under par for the first time ever in my golfing career." He poked Dallas's foot again with his pen. "I've booked a theatre. Your persistence paid off Mrs. Hellson. This break here," he pointed to a spot just below Dallas's knee, "broke cleanly but is pushing against the main artery. Any longer and your husband might have lost the use of his foot."

I clenched my jaw, and stared down at Dallas's beautiful face. He would have hated that.

"Don't worry, Mrs Hellson. I'll have Dallas

dancing an Irish jig by Christmas. This will take few hours, so I suggest you take a break. " With that, he strode out of the room.

Jake Thorne must have lived up to his rockstar ego, because within minutes someone was there to wheel Dallas down to surgery.

Without Dallas to focus on, I took a good hard look at Ruben. He was holding himself wrong somehow. I narrowed my eyes. It was his arm.

"What's wrong with your arm?" I closed the distance between us and pulled up his sleeve. His wrist was a mass of deep purple bruises. "Has someone taken a look at that?"

Ruben shook his head. "Wasn't time."

"There's time now."

After the nurses assured me that they would call me as soon as they knew anything, I walked with Ruben to sit in the ER. He called everyone to let them know Dallas' status. Ida was minding Iris, and Elise was minding Ida. They were a little worried that the stress might be too much for the aging Hellson matriarch.

Wyatt was dealing with the insurance, and the inspectors who had to come out and look at the warehouse after a workplace accident. Liz and Helen were on their way out from New York.

I was not sure I was in the right frame of mind for that reunion.

In a surprisingly short time, probably because the triage nurse thought Ruben was attractive, Ruben was in being seen by a doctor. An X-ray later, we discovered that Ruben had fractured his arm close to the wrist, but it was a clean break and easily mended with a plaster cast and some pain meds.

We went back up to the ICU, but there was still no word from theatre. We sat in the ICU waiting room and stared at the wall.

Slowly people arrived. Wyatt, Elise and Ida came together, Baba and Ted taking over Iris's babysitting. Some of the guys from the carnival, who had been helping during the unload, drifted in for a time to lean against the walls like gargoyles.

Finally, Liz and Helen arrived from New York. Helen was almost an exact clone for Elise, except the Hellson baby blues. She walked up and hugged Ruben, then her parents enveloped her in their arms.

Elizabeth stood back, staring at her feet.

"Liz." Ruben's deep voice carried around the room. The girl's head snapped up and Ruben opened his arms. Liz rushed into them like a lost puppy.

"I'm sorry," I heard her whisper, but Ruben just shook his head.

"We can talk about it later."

"Any updates on Dallas?"

Ruben shook his head. And that was it. She didn't even ask where Iris was, or if she was okay.

I turned away from them before I snapped and opened my mouth.

Elise came to sit beside me. "How are you holding up?" She patted my back in soothing circles.

"I'm fine. Worried to death."

"He'll be fine. He's a tough young man. I hear you and Dallas got married?"

The sound sucked out of the room and everyone turned toward me.

"In Vegas, by Elvis. It was on the list. We were going to get it annulled when we left Nevada."

A man cleared his throat. "Well, I'm glad you didn't. It would have made getting access to your trust fund nigh on impossible until you were twenty-five."

I whipped around. "Frederick!"

I bolted out of the chair and wrapped my arms around the aging lawyer. He whooshed out a little air, and then made some slightly embarrassed noises. I pulled away.

"I'm sorry. I'm just so glad you came."

"Well, ah, there are things you needed to sign and uh, you sounded as if you could use the support."

"Well, thank you."

Another masculine voice cleared. Ruben was up out of his seat. "How'd it go, Doc?"

Doctor Thorne raised his eyes at Ruben's sky blue plaster cast, but his face quickly assumed a mask of cool professionalism.

"The surgery was a success. I put in two plates and sixteen pins, but he should be fine with some physio and time. I don't believe in guardian angels, but if those poles went half an inch higher, he'd be singing soprano. I'd start with a slow Irish jig," he said to me. "He'll be out of post op and back in ICU within the hour."

I reached out and shook the doctor's hand. "Thank you, Doctor Thorne. I'm sorry for doubting your prowess."

"Don't thank me just yet. You haven't seen my bill."

"Worth every cent, I know."

With another bemused but still condescending smile, he left.

I let out the breath I'd been holding since Ruben called earlier today. Or was it yesterday? Dallas wasn't out of the woods yet, but he was getting there.

I waited until everyone else had seen Dallas. Everyone needed to reassure themselves that he was okay. Frederick waited with me, typing out emails on his phone.

"I'll handle your annulment when you're ready," he said, not looking up from his phone. "Did, err, Elvis make you sign anything I should know about?"

I couldn't help but laugh. "I signed a prenup, if that's what you mean."

"Oh good." He continued typing on his phone. "How did you go with your friends list?"

"I completed it, kind of. All... Wait how do you know about Angela's bucket list?"

He reached into the inside pocket of his Brooks Brothers suit jacket, and pulled out an envelope. My name was written on it in Angela's handwriting.

"Your friend was quite the character. She called me up and asked me to give this to you once you had completed the list, or if I thought you needed it. I could hardly say no."

"Why you? Why not her parents, or my parents? She hardly knew you."

He shrugged, an innocuous gesture on a man in his late sixties.

"I must have made quite the impression after the fencing snail's conversation. I was glad she did. I enjoyed our short acquaintance, and I was happy to do my part in fulfilling a dying girl's final wish."

I ran my fingers along the teenage scrawl of Angela's handwriting. She'd always been too impatient to have decent penmanship, or so said Mrs. Ryskowski of fourth grade.

I put it in my purse. I couldn't read it now. "Thanks, Frederick."

He stood, and rested his hand on my shoulder. "I hope your young man recovers soon. But I best go to my hotel. Come by the Hyatt when you can and we'll sign all the necessary paperwork to release your trust. Did you happen to look how much your grandparents had left you?"

I shook my head. In all honesty, I'd pushed the contracts into a drawer as soon as Frederick had left me in Prairieville and not thought of it since.

"Your grandparents died almost thirty years ago, and as your parents had no other offspring you get the entire amount. There is over twelve million dollars in that account. I suggest you don't go spending it thoughtlessly, and use your parents trust for all your schooling, and it should last you many, many years."

Oh my freaking god. I was loaded.

Frederick didn't have to worry. I wasn't about to spend it frivolously on fancy cars and renting private islands. Being rich had never done a thing for me, but living hard this summer had helped me discover who I really was. But I appreciated that it gave me the option to do and be whatever I wanted.

Ida, Wyatt, Elise, Helen pushed through the security door to ICU. "You can go in. Ruben is still in there. See if you can't get him to go home and rest. We are heading back to the big house," Elise said.

I gave them all a tight smile and a quick goodbye.

"I shall leave with you, if you would not mind the company," Frederick asked.

"You are more than welcome to join us," Ida said, giving him a watery smile.

I walked into ICU as quietly as I could. It was late and visiting hours were over, but I just needed to see him.

Ruben stood above him in the dull light of the night lamp. He was holding Dallas' hand and saying something in a low, soft voice that I couldn't catch. The moment looked so tender, I didn't want to interrupt so I stood by the nurse's desk. The night nurse came over, a round, strong woman with beautiful skin the color of coffee. But she had a serious case of resting bitch face.

But when she spoke, she had the softest voice I'd ever heard. It was a balm. "They make quite a picture. I keep having to shoo my nurses so they actually get some work done, else they just stand here and moon at your boys."

They did seem awfully angelic in that light.

"How long until they bring him around?"

"Tomorrow they'll lower the meds and let him rise to consciousness, if they are happy with his brain pressure that is. If they are happy with his neural responses, they'll wake him up completely. If they aren't, they'll put him back under." She bustled around, writing notes into the computer. "Get the big one to go home. He's cramping up my workplace." Her words were harsh, but I could pick up a hint of mirth in her tone.

Ruben looked up, and I walked over to the hospital bed. Dallas was strung up like a marionette, his legs held in metal cages. I leaned over and kissed his lips, which were dry and cracked.

"The nurse said they'd try to wake him up tomorrow," I whispered. Ruben just nodded. "We need to go."

His jaw tensed. I didn't want to leave either. "You need to sleep and I need you to take me home. I don't know where you live."

He looked wrung out. Maybe I'd drive.

Ruben sighed. He squeezed the hand he was holding. "Love you kid." He turned to me. "Let's go."

I leaned down and kissed his cheek. "I love you, too."

It felt wrong leaving him there by himself. But neither one of us would be any good to him passed out on the ICU floor from exhaustion.

We rode in silence down to the ground floor. "I came in the ambulance. We'll need to take a cab."

I didn't think either of us was capable of keeping our eyes open for long enough to even get home anyway. We'd just have ended up in ICU in matching beds to Dallas.

We slid into the hailed cab, and I couldn't help but draw comparisons to the last time we were in the back of a car together.

"Well, at least neither of us are in cuffs this time."

Ruben huffed out a laugh. "Silver lining. Nights still young though."

"You cracked a joke. Holy hell, you must be exhausted to the point of delirium."

He just smirked and we fell into silence. I watched the unfamiliar streets rush by, toward a home that wasn't my own, but one filled with people I loved anyway.

"Why didn't you guys tell me you were eloping?" he sounded hurt. That was almost as weird as him cracking jokes.

"You know Dallas and his surprises. I didn't even know until he was pulling up in front of the chapel and handing me a dress. Besides, what would you have said?"

"I would have said that you were great for each

other, you are like a matching pair. You ground him, and he helps you be crazy and free."

"And?"

"And that you are way too young to even contemplate getting married."

"Exactly. But honestly, it wasn't meant to stick. We were going to get it annulled the next day."

Ruben gave me a long appraisal, kind of like the one he gave me the first day we met.

"But it didn't work out like that and here we are."

"As Dallas would say, it's kismet."

Ruben made a non-committal sound and went back to staring out the window.

CHAPTER EIGHTEEN

PASADENA, CALIFORNIA

I woke up in an unfamiliar bed, the light of the sun from the open window enough to rouse me from a dreamless sleep. I woke to the smell of Dallas' cologne on my pillow, and my first urge was to look for him before reality took me in her firm grasp.

I looked around the room, taking in the royal blue walls, and the white shabby chic furniture. I was in a California king bed that I could almost lie on diagonally without touching the edges.

A framed sketch hung on the wall. It was a scene from the carnival in full swing, from just inside the midway. It was beautifully done and painstakingly rendered. Down in the corner was Dallas initials.

I stood up, grabbing one of Dallas's hoodies from the chair where it had been thrown. I breathed in his scent as I put it over my head. I shuffled over to the dresser.

On top of white wooden chest of drawers was a framed picture of his family, and it was the first time I'd ever seen a picture of his parents. He was a nearly exact mold of his father, only his father was built more like Ruben. Tall, large and imposing, however he seemed to temper it with a large, happy smile.

His mother was also tall, her arms wrapped around a very young Liz. She had high cheekbones that hinted at a bit of Native American heritage and straight dark hair that fell to her waist. Her dark eyes crinkled at the corners from laughter.

A prepubescent Dallas and a teenage Ruben capped off the photo, their smiles large. It was a beautiful photo.

I don't think I'd ever had any photos taken with my parents. Actually, hardly any photos hung in my house at all. One of Mother getting an award for some discovery that prevented a parasite found in the water of third world countries from staying in the body. One of Father being made partner, shaking the hand of an equally stern man. That was about it. My entire childhood, before I met Angela anyway, would always be a blank. No baby photos to show my kids, or pictures of my first steps, or my first day of school.

Angela's parents had loads of us growing up, though. Though they would stop now too.

I took in the rest of the dresser's contents. A few more photos, most of a smiling Dallas with various people. With Wyatt and Elise and his cousins, one of the whole extended family including Baba and Ted. There was a pile of change and on the very corner was his wedding ring. I picked it up and slid it onto my thumb. It was just a plain silver band, but it had meant something when I'd slipped it on his finger. It was way too big, even for my thumb, so I went to my duffle and pulled a long chain from my beauty case. Threading the ring on, I put it under my jumper so it could rest between my breasts, right beside my heart.

I pulled out the flower crown and my bouquet from my bag. They'd been in their clear protective boxes when I'd shoved them in there, so they weren't too banged up. With the ribbon from the box I hung my bouquet from the curtain rod upside down so they could dry. I did the same for my flower crown. Once they'd dried I'd put them back in their protective boxes, but it would take a while. Hopefully Dallas wouldn't mind.

I didn't remember much about last night after I fell asleep in the cab, but I had a vague recollection of climbing stairs. I looked down a long hall. There were three doors on either side of the hallway, Dallas's being the closest one to the stairs.

When I got downstairs, I followed the smell of food. I walked into the kitchen to find Baba cooking. Actually, judging by the massive piles of pastries, cakes, cookies and breads on the bench, Baba had been doing a lot of cooking.

Baba turned a smiling face to me, and seeing my gob smacked expression, she shrugged. "If I am upset, I cook." Her polish accent gets stronger too, apparently. "Now eat. How long since you eat? One day? Two?"

I'd had a steady stream of coffee, but I didn't think Baba counted that.

I picked up a Danish, and a hot roll. Slathering the roll with butter, I sat down on one of the stools tucked under the breakfast bar. I looked at the clock on the wall. It wasn't even eight yet.

"Is everyone still asleep?" I asked Baba. Baba always got up at four am to begin breakfast prep. Apparently it was a habit that carried over to her civilian life.

She shook her head. "Ruben is in the garage constructing wheelchair ramps."

I picked up another roll and Danish, putting them on a plate. Pouring a large mug of coffee, I followed Baba's directions to the garage.

It must have been soundproofed in some way, because I didn't hear the sound of the circular saw until I was right at the door.

I knocked, and walked in. I was pretty sure Ruben didn't use power tools naked.

He had been busy. There were at least six ramps of varying length leaning up against the garage door.

He gave me a small wave of greeting.

"I brought you some breakfast. I figured you'd been living on coffee too, and at least one of us should be spared from Baba's disapproval. Should you be doing that with a broken arm?"

He shrugged. "I can make it work one-handed."

Obviously, but I doubted he was doing his arm any favors by using it.

"When do you want to head back to the hospital?" I doubted he'd had more than two hours sleep judging by all the ramps he'd completed already.

"Visiting hours aren't until ten."

"I can pull my rich bitch act and get us in there early if you want. Money has to be good for something."

He gave me a half smile, and nodded. "Give me half an hour to clean up."

I hesitated at the door. "You should eat." Then I hightailed it out of there before he could growl at me.

I asked Baba where the bathroom was because it seemed like a safer option than randomly opening doors. I was halfway up the stairs when Liz started to come down. Dammit. I totally would have hidden at the bottom if I'd known. I squared my shoulders

"Morning." I went to step around her but she stood in my way.

"Are you going to the hospital?"

I nodded.

"Can I catch a ride with you?"

Forty minutes in the car with Liz. Sounded like about as much fun as letting Ruben do a circular saw lobotomy on me. "Uh, sure. We leave in 25 minutes."

"I just wanted to say I'm sorry."

Awkward. "It's fine. I'm not really the person you should be apologizing to. Besides, this isn't really the right time." With that, I stepped around her and strode into the bathroom.

THE LONGEST CAR ride of my life later, I was completely caught up on Liz's life as she spoke with Ruben in the front of Aunt Ida's VW.

She'd been seeing a psychologist, working through her parent's death and Jonas' abandonment. The psych had suggested she go back to school, so she was taking a hairdressing course at the community college. She also got a job at Walmart to help Helen with the bills. She was doing much better by all accounts, except not once had she mentioned Iris. Even as she talked through her progress regarding Jonas, she didn't say a word about Iris.

I could tell Ruben also noticed, because although he was nodding and murmuring all positive things, his jaw was tense.

I managed to get us into ICU early by shamelessly name dropping Doctor Thorne's name. The night nurse with the RBF was still there and gave us a tired nod as we went in.

Luckily, we were met there by the neurosurgeon on his morning rounds. He looked like a stereotypical doctor fortunately; greying, white coat and stethoscope, manicured hands, the whole deal.

"Are you going to wake him up?"

The surgeon looked at the chart in his hands. "His vitals all look good, so I think we will. The longer he's in an induced coma, the more complicated it will be when we bring him out of it."

He showed the chart to the two other doctors with him, or maybe they were medical students, and they all made notes.

"Okay, let's wake him up. Nurse?" The nurse removed the long tube from his throat and I resisted the urge to gag. It reminded me of the magician's trick where they keep pulling scarves from their sleeve and it appears that it's never ending. The tube was really long. The room held its breath, but he continued to breathe fine on his own.

The nurse fiddled with his drip, and then if by magic, Dallas' eyes opened. There was an audible sigh of relief around the room.

The doctor leaned over, shining a light in his eyes.

"Hey there, Son. Do you know your name?"

"Dallas," his voice was hoarse. "Water?" The nurse put a straw to his lips, gently removing it after only a small sip.

"Do you know what year it is?"

I held my breath after each question.

"2018."

"What's the last thing you remember?"

"Getting dressed for work."

"Do you recognize the people at the end of the bed?" Dallas stared at us, blinking to clear his eyes.

"My brother, Ruben. My sister, Liz," he stared at me long and hard. The silence dragged on, and I could feel my heart breaking. "My wife, Livvy."

A weird, choked-up sob gurgled from my throat. "Hey there." I gave him a large watery smile. He was fine. His brain was fine. His legs would heal. My knees felt weak and I clutched the end of the bed.

"How long have you been married for?" The doctor asked, testing his reflexes, poking him in the fingers, squeezing his toes.

"What day is it?"

"Friday," the nurse answered.

"Five days."

The surgeon laughed. "Well, this isn't much of a honeymoon then."

I laughed like it was the funniest thing I'd ever heard; relief had made me giddy.

The surgeon jabbed his pen into the foot that Doctor Thorne said he'd almost lost. "It tickles a bit."

The group of doctors made notes.

"That's good. There's been some nerve damage, but you'll recover more feeling in time. You are lucky you had Doctor Thorne. Quite the boy-genius that one." He quirked an eyebrow at me. Apparently, my rudeness had gotten around.

"I'm happy for you to remain awake. But you need lots of rest," that one was directed toward the end of the bed. "But I don't think you've suffered any lasting ill effects from the bang to the head or the surgery. We'll keep a close eye of you for the next week or so, just in case. I'll send you down for another scan today. "

He took more notes and talked to the med students in indecipherable medical jargon. Then they left. Ruben and Liz rushed to Dallas's side. They both talked at once, becoming a garbled mess of relief.

He answered their questions, although he still seemed a little spaced out. Finally, he looked to the end of the bed.

"Come here, Livvy."

Ruben stepped away so I could hold his hand. I leaned in and kissed his lips.

"I was so scared. I love you so much," I whispered against his mouth. I was going to tell him how much I loved him every chance I got.

"Sorry. Don't cry."

I pulled back a little, and realized the tears running down his cheeks were mine. I swiped at them with the back of my arms.

"I thought I'd lost you too."

"Never," he said as his eyes closed and he went off to sleep.

He is okay, I told my aching heart.

I sat beside him, taking the first shift sitting with him. I hated the idea of him being alone in hospital now that he was awake. The chair was so hard that my ass was numb already but the peaceful look on his face was worth it.

I remembered the letter Frederick had given me the night before, still tucked safely away in my bag.

Taking it out, I opened the seal gently. I pulled the thick, beautiful paper from the heavy envelope and unfolded it. Angela had always had a hard on for good stationary, and this was no exception. Taking a deep breath, I began to read.

Dear Livvy,

If you are reading this, I am dead.

How cool is that? I mean, how many people get to have a total Vincent Price moment? Maybe I could convince Freddy to grow a pencil mustache and read this out to you in a spooky voice. I mean, who can say no to a dying girl?

But seriously, if you are reading this, I'm dead and you've finished the bucket list. Well done, Livvy, I am so proud of you. I knew there was an adventurer in there, behind the walls of your fortress of solitude. There's just one thing, Livvy. One thing that I hope you've worked out for yourself, because you are the smartest, most beautiful person I know. But maybe you haven't because you're a little emotionally dense. That's not your fault. Your parents are assholes. I can say that now because I'm dead. I hate your parents. So, so much. I tried not to say that when I was alive because I still had to see them all the time. But I can tell you, there's a special place in hell for parents who treated their children the way yours treated you. Not that I'd know. I'm totally in the other place.

Back to the point.

The bucket list was never my bucket list, Livvy. It was yours.

I knew when I died, you would close yourself away. You'd become the good little automaton your parents wanted, because loving someone can hurt so, so badly. I didn't want that for you. I wanted you to live. I couldn't help my parents; no matter what I could say or write, they will mourn me until the end of their days, and that is a heavy burden for me to bear.

But you are different. I could help you from beyond the grave. With your overactive sense of responsibility, I knew if I asked you to do this thing for me, you would. Because you'd always help me, even if you wouldn't help yourself.

I'm writing this letter because I love you. I always wanted a sister, and then fate dropped you into my lap (if fate was Madison Krawley and my lap was the sandbox I was sitting in. Madison Krawley is still a bitch by the way). You have been the best sister I could have ever asked for, and I don't think I ever told you I love you enough. And I knew if you just had the opportunity to spread your wings, you could really soar.

So on this cliché, I am closing out this letter. Just know, you were the most amazing friend anyone could ever have asked for. Don't close yourself off to love. It's what makes living worth it.

Eternally yours (and probably haunting you from beyond the grave),

Angela xo

P. S yes, it is me that keeps making all your picture frames uneven and hiding your keys.

"And then the Adventurer nursed the White Knight back to health, and they moved into a big castle right next door to the beautiful princess, and everyone lived happily ever after. The end."

The little girl beneath the unicorn duvet let out a deep, contented sigh.

"That's my favorite story ever," she said, though her voice was muffled from the four layer deep pile of stuffed toys in her bed.

"Mine too." I smiled at Iris, kissing her forehead beneath her soft curls. I removed all of the stuffed animals slowly, placing them in the oversized blanket box at the end of the four poster bed. Dallas and I babysat a lot, and it made sense for Iris to have her own room in our house. Plus, it was fun to decorate a little girl's room the way I would have wanted it as a child.

"I wanna come to the party!" Iris's bottom lip jutted out for the sixth time since she'd put on her pajamas.

"I know, maybe next time." I leaned forward conspiratorially. "How about I put a movie on your TV?"

I struggled not to smile at her shocked gasp. "Before sleepy time? Daddy says I'm not allowed to do that. That it'll melt my brain and turn my eyes square," she whispered.

"It's a special occasion, I'm sure he won't mind. And your eyes and brain will be fine just this one time."

Iris had called Ruben Daddy from the time she could talk. It made him melt every single time. It was adorable. He and Maja got married when Iris was two, and the love that the three of them had for each other was visible to anyone who spent two minutes in their presence.

"I wanna watch Cindy. I like her pretty dress when she gets married at the end. Will you and Uncle Dally ever get married? I wanna be a flower girl like Teeni was."

There was a strangled laugh from the doorway, and I looked over to see Dallas holding in a serious case of the giggles. God, he still made me feel giddy when I looked at him. Technically, we were actually still married. It just seemed easier to stay married back then, with the endless operations and physical therapy to get Dallas back on his feet taking up all our spare time. We didn't have time for lawyers and petitions for divorce. That first year we fought a lot, though. He was in pain and I was constantly commuting to and from school, and we were both just exhausted. But at no point during the yelling, and the hurt feelings, and the apologies, did I ever think about calling Frederick to get a divorce.

"Maybe one day, Little One. Livvy would make a beautiful bride, don't you think?"

"The prettiest!"

The opening credits for Cinderella began to play, and we snuck out of the room as Iris became transfixed.

Walking down the curving staircase, we followed the sound of laughter. Dallas curved his arm around my waist, leaning in to kiss my temple as we walked into the dining room, where the party was in full swing.

"Love you," he murmured in my ear.

I smiled up at him. "Always."

I looked down the long table that took up most of the formal dining room, handmade by Ruben

Hellson himself. It easily seated the twenty people in the room, and had taken Ruben two years to make, the perfect housewarming gift for when Dallas and I had settled our house.

The party was like a highlight reel of my life so far. Frederick was there, as well as Lindy and Tom, Angela's parents. I'm sure Angela was too, if only in spirit. Lindy and Tom had been coming to visit me on the West Coast every winter since I started school, although they still looked a little sad at these events.

Across from them sat Aunt Ida and Tommy, the tattooist from Odessa. I still stopped in to see Tommy every year over summer with the carnival, and he came out to visit for the West Coast Tattoo Convention every year.

Wyatt and Elise had just returned from their winter home in Florida. It was nice to have them back. They sat beside Baba and Ted, who had come for the occasion, and Baba was telling Lucy and Aurelia, my friends from school, all about how she and Ted met. Ted was dozing in the chair, as usual. Manny sat beside him, talking to Maja, who sat with her hands resting on her baby bump.

J sat beside Ruben, talking about design. The architect and the craftsman. Ruben had taken my advice and seized the day. He and Maja had come to an agreement, splitting the year between Mexico and Cali, before getting married three years ago. Ruben smiled so much now that he was getting permanent crow's feet. Maja had adopted Iris straight after, without any contesting from Liz. Liz had a whole life in New York now, and she was happy just being Aunt Liz who visited at Christmas with the other aunts.

Dallas and I sat at opposite ends of the table, chatting to guests, reminiscing with old friends and catching up with new ones.

Three glasses of wine later, Dallas stood at the other end of the table, tapping his beer bottle with a knife. He was all class, that one.

"Can I have everyone's attention please?" he asked and the crowd quieted down. "Thank you all for coming here to help celebrate Livvy's acceptance into medical school. Not that there was any doubt in my mind that she would get in, because she's as smart as she is beautiful. And more stubborn than any person I have ever met, and I lived with Ruben for twenty years." Everyone laughed, and Ruben swung a half-hearted punch at Dallas's stomach. "I know we both feel extremely lucky to have so many people in our life who are always there to share in the good times and the bad. So thank you again." He raised his bottle. "To Olivia, who will be the most amazing pediatric oncologist the country has ever seen."

"To Olivia," everyone repeated as they all raised their glasses toward me. Tears gathered in the corners of my eyes and I blinked them away quickly.

I raised my glass and smiled. I looked to Lindy and Tom, who were both close to tears.

"To Angela, without her friendship and love, I would not be where I am now and would never have found such happiness."

Glasses around the table clinked.

"To Angela."

A NOTE FROM THE AUTHOR

Thank you for reading. I hope you enjoyed running away with the carnival as much as I enjoyed writing about it.

I love hearing from readers, so you can find me at any of these places below:

Facebook Author Page: https://www.facebook.com/GraceMcGintyAuthor/

Instagram: @gracemcgintyauthor

Website: www.gracemcginty.com

Twitter: @McgintyGrace

Email: gracemcgintyauthor@gmail.com

And now for the battle cry of all indie authors. If you liked this book, or any book, leave a review, or recommend it to a friend, or write the Amazon link on the wall of a bathroom stall.

Anything helps, and it keeps indie writers creating the stories you love so much.

CPSIA information can be obtained
at www.ICGtesting.com
Printed in the USA
LVHW041111040219
606286LV00003BA/235/P